Deadlocked

Also by Richard Hunt

Death of a Merry Widow

DEADLOCKED

Richard Hunt

St. Martin's Press
New York

Library of Congress Cataloging-in-Publication Data

Hunt, Richard
Deadlocked / by Richard Hunt.
p. cm.
ISBN 0-312-13461-4 (hardcover)
1. Police—England—Cambridge—Fiction.
2. Cambridge (England)—Fiction.   I. Title.
PR6058.U517D4   1995
823'.914—dc20   95-23731   CIP

First published in Great Britain by
Constable & Company, Ltd.

First U.S. Edition: December 1995
10 9 8 7 6 5 4 3 2 1

Deadlocked

1

As the back of his car started to slide for the second time, Mervyn Grigson again swung the wheel deftly to correct the drift, but this time he took his foot right off the accelerator, and changed down into second gear. In these conditions he'd have to go dead slow, and hope things got no worse.

This journey was becoming a bit of a nightmare. It had merely been raining when he'd left Scotland, yesterday afternoon. That had been bad enough, what with all the spray and the lights of oncoming cars turning the smeary windscreen into a dangerous mass of opaque streaks. The motorway from Carlisle had been no better. The traffic had been heavy, as was to be expected on a Friday night, with people like him making their way home for the weekend.

In the Midlands though, as he'd started to travel eastwards, that rain had turned to driving sleet that beat a steady tattoo on the windscreen, and even with the wipers going flat out, visibility had dropped from poor to damned awful. He'd hoped the weather might improve while he stopped at the motorway service station, but it hadn't.

He wasted no more than a plegmatic shoulder-shrug at the conditions, however, as he drove on eastwards, through the winding country roads of Northamptonshire. To a sales representative like him, his car was a second home and the controls part of his physical make-up. Moaning about the weather was a waste of time, one accepted whatever came without complaint.

Nevertheless it had come as a surprise when he'd suddenly

driven out of that sleety rain into a scene of eerie white peace and tranquillity.

The rolling countryside lay deadly still under a thin layer of snow, like some gigantic Christmas card. Even the road noise from the tyres changed to a whispering hush in this magical unreal world.

This was Cambridgeshire now, and Grigson was nearly home, well, he was within ten miles or so, but it was no time to start relaxing, for the road was treacherously slippery, and a light squally wind was blowing soft white flakes on to his windscreen. The so useful 'cat's-eyes' in the middle of the road had completely disappeared, but there were the faint tracks of an earlier vehicle to follow.

Tired though he was, Grigson concentrated on keeping the car in the middle of the road, straddling the camber. That was the safest place to be, and at nearly two o'clock in the morning, there was no other traffic. He hadn't seen another car for at least a quarter of an hour.

He kept going slowly.

Suddenly, he came to the ring road that guarded the western approaches to the city of Cambridge. Under so many high street lights, he could now see quite well, and it was just a case of driving through the unnaturally white and silent city roads and out a few miles on the other side, to the village of Fulbourn, and his warm comfortable home. He would creep in without disturbing his wife and two children - a welcome could wait until the morning.

The long narrow lane from the village was thickly wooded on one side, and had high hedges shielding the houses on the other.

Grigson could relax now as he studied the bank of hedges, looking for the gap that was the entrance to his own drive, and thus was unprepared when he was suddenly blinded by the headlights of a vehicle that had swung out into the road ahead of him.

There was no time to think. He swung the wheel sharply and accelerated, to try and avoid a head-on collision.

In that respect, he was successful, but his reward was rather

6

unkind: he crashed into his own front gatepost, and came to an abrupt jarring halt. That was immediately followed by another bone-shaking sideways crunch, as the other vehicle rammed his rear off-side.

Though he was numbed momentarily by the impact that had jerked him forward against his seat-belt, Grigson's shock turned slowly into anger. He'd driven nearly four hundred miles, only to crash at his own front gate – he who had had no accident in the last ten years. His fingers clenched into fists that pounded the steering wheel in a wild feeling of anger and hatred against the driver of that other vehicle, which had continued on its way without stopping.

That vehicle had come from his neighbour's house.

It was hardly the time to go visiting, but that thought did not cross Grigson's mind; there was only a compelling desire to find out the name of that car's driver, and vent his spleen on someone – anyone.

He eased himself out of his car and set off, a little unsteadily, down the road, his shoes crunching the soft melting snow as he went. Even in this dimly lit lane there was sufficient light to see reasonably well: the whiteness of the snow seemed to create its own illumination.

A chest-high steel-meshed gate barred the way to his neighbour's drive, and Grigson's fumbling fingers could find no catch. Dimly, he realized that the car tracks did not go past the gate, the vehicle had only turned in the entrance, churning up the snow into deep ruts, but there were footprints on the other side, going across the front lawn towards a lighted ground-floor window. That lighted window obviously meant that the owner of the house was still up and about.

Grigson clambered over the gate, digging his toes into the mesh for footholds, quite heedless of the risk of damage to his neat suit, and strode up the drive and along to the front door. He was startled when a spotlight, high on the wall above, came on to blind him momentarily, but he ignored it, and jabbed firmly at the door-bell button, holding it down long and hard. He could hear it jangling within the house.

He rang again, and then again, but there were no responding sounds or signs of life.

All of a sudden he became aware of the chill in the air and a dampness at his feet, and he started pacing about impatiently, swinging his arms, but still no one came to answer his summons.

Then he thought of the lighted window.

If the owner was in that room, he could bang on the glass to attract his attention. He went along to the front of the house.

The window curtains were drawn back, and he could see into the room quite clearly.

The beige leather three-piece suite held no occupants, nor was anyone standing, but there was someone there, all the same.

That someone lay on its back, still and motionless, before the dead or dying embers in the ornate white marble fireplace, but what caused Grigson's second violent shock of the morning was the fact that plunged into the man's chest was a bronze-coloured sword, with twinkling coloured stones set jewel-like round the ruby-red pommel. There was a dark ominous stain on the white sweater round the blade.

Grigson blinked his tired eyes and stared, swallowing hard on a throat suddenly dry and parched, but those involuntary actions changed the visual picture not one iota.

It took some moments for Grigson's mind to accept that he was really seeing what he was looking at, but when that comprehension came, it brought a gasp of near-panic, and sent Grigson running frantically away, to clamber back over the gate, and to slip and slide to his stricken vehicle, there to ring 999 on his car phone.

To ring the 999 emergency service is a straightforward enough thing to do, provided the caller is thinking reasonably clearly, but Grigson's mind at that time was anything but clear. After what seemed to him an age in time, he was put through to the police, and to his dismay found that he was expected to repeat his story, and add more detail.

Anything unusual in an emergency message does tend to create a certain suspicion in the official mind, because hoaxes are all too frequent. Mervyn Grigson's story was unusual; so the duty sergeant at Police Headquarters persisted in his politely worded questioning. Having been told Grigson's full name and address, he asked for Grigson's telephone number. That number had a radio-phone prefix however, and so prompted another question.

'So, you're at home, sir, are you? At this address in Badon Lane, Fulbourn, but you're outside using your car phone. What's your car number?' the sergeant asked, then he put his hand over the mouthpiece and called out to one of the others in the office, 'Which car's nearest to Fulbourn? Get them on the radio, will you? Tell them to stand by.'

'Yes, that's right,' Grigson replied, having stated his car number automatically. 'I was nearly home when this damned fool of a driver came hurtling out of my neighbour's drive, straight at me. Made me hit my own bloody gatepost, and he crunched my back end, but look here, this has got nothing to do with it, I'm telling you there's a body in the next –'

'So, you've been in a motor accident as well, have you? Anyone hurt? Are you sure you're all right?'

'Of course I am. I'd have asked for a damned ambulance if I wasn't, wouldn't I? Listen! This next-door neighbour of mine, at least I think it's him, he's got this ruddy great bronze sword sticking in his chest . . . I keep telling you. Are you going to do something about it?'

'". . . ruddy great bronze sword sticking in his chest." Right, Mr Grigson, you stay where you are. A police car will be with you in just a few minutes.'

'Stay where I am? No, I bloody well won't! It's freezing cold out here. I'm going indoors.' Grigson slammed the phone down on the passenger seat in frustration. Suddenly he felt dizzy and exhausted. He staggered uneasily over the fallen gatepost and up the drive to his house, fumbling for his door

9

key. He now felt quite sick and had a desperately urgent need to use the toilet.

The duty sergeant pulled at his chin thoughtfully. The details of Grigson's car had already come up on the monitor screen before him. It wasn't registered in the name of Grigson, but in the name of a well-known London publishing company. The man's speech had been noticeably slurred – possibly he was a drunk and his story the creation of an alcohol-abused mind, but two thirty in the morning was a bit late for one of those, and reps were rare drink-drivers. Nevertheless, a murder, or at least an unauthorized killing, had been reported, and there were standing orders to be followed in such an eventuality. CID and the Scene of Crime section must be alerted immediately.

The sergeant looked at his watch. The patrol car would confirm things one way or another within ten minutes or so, but to those in uniform the CID and SOC were a right cocky bunch, always expecting others to jump to it and run around for them whenever they demanded.

The CID's big white chief would be fast asleep in his comfortable bed right now, and not be pleased at being disturbed, particularly when in ten minutes or so the Grigson call might, indeed probably would, turn out to be a hoax – ruddy great bronze sword and all.

Under those circumstances some duty sergeants might feel justified in waiting a few moments before disturbing other people's rest, but on the other hand, orders were orders.

There was definitely a malicious grin on this duty sergeant's face as he reached for the phone.

The big white chief of the Cambridgeshire Constabulary's Criminal Investigation Department was Detective Chief Inspector Sidney James Walsh. He was in his early fifties, a confident, ruggedly handsome, six-foot man with appropriately greying hair and a slightly thickened left ear lobe, the result of a penalty-awarding high tackle in his rugby-playing days. His face generally bore the serious expression common to most CID officers, but he could smile readily enough at times, and then his shrewd brown eyes would twinkle with humour.

The duty sergeant was wrong in thinking that this big white chief would be peacefully asleep in his comfortable bed. Sidney Walsh was tossing and turning restlessly.

Before turning in for the night he had been talking to his wife, Gwen, who was thousands of miles away, in a hotel in the United States. She was on a biannual two-week tour for the children's book publishing company of which she was a director. She had only been gone three days, yet Walsh was already missing her more than he cared to admit. Sure, he could look after himself, that was no problem, but Gwen was more than just a wife, she was a friend and lover as well, and the house seemed cold and empty without her presence. They'd talked for a long while, the cost of the phone bill was irrelevant, but he was finding it impossible to get to sleep.

So the duty sergeant found that his call was answered surprisingly promptly.

'This chap says the sword is bronze and has coloured stones set round the pommel?' Walsh replied. 'They're not the kind of details you get in a drunk's story. You've alerted the Scene of Crime team?'

The sergeant had.

'Right, there's no need to panic then,' Walsh went on. 'I'll hang on until the patrol car reports back.'

But by the time Grigson's story had been confirmed, Walsh was already fully dressed.

'Badon Lane, Fulbourn, you say? Ring Phipps and Finch, tell them to meet me there,' he instructed, as he put the phone down.

Detective Constable Brenda Phipps and Detective Sergeant Reginald Finch made up his Serious Crime team. It sounded as though he would need them with him.

Now, Walsh thought, if he hurried and got there before all the Forensic team arrived, he might just be able to do a bit of

11

scouting around the area on his own, before too many clumsy feet had destroyed whatever tracks there were.

Good intentions were one thing; fate had other ideas.

Having swept the windows of his car clear of the light coating of snow, he found that it would not start. There was damp in the ignition, or a blockage in the fuel pipe, or something else that would not respond to the insistent use of the starter motor. Only the battery started – to protest.

Walsh gave it up in favour of his wife's car, safe from the elements in the garage, but before he could use that, he needed to push his own car out of the drive and go back in the house for the keys.

While he was there he made himself a flask of hot coffee to take with him, for by then his desire for haste had ebbed away.

It is ironic that the Investigating Officer, even though he may be in charge of a subsequent murder inquiry, is in a peculiar position, initially, at the actual scene of a crime; for it is the leader of the Forensic team who is in command of the situation there. It is his and their task, not the CID's, to ensure that all the evidence is preserved and collected. Until that is done to their satisfaction, they have the statutory power, in order to prevent evidence being damaged, distorted or contaminated, to restrict access to the site by non-specialists, whoever they are, be they Detective Chief Inspectors, or even Chief Constables.

Although such confrontations are possible, they are almost unheard of. All the professionals concerned need to co-operate and work closely together, and that means avoiding the proverbial treading on of toes.

Since none of the many specialists in the Forensic team had made flasks of coffee before leaving home in cars that had started first time, it was hardly surprising that Badon Lane, Fulbourn, was already quite a hive of activity when the Investigating Officer, Detective Chief Inspector Sidney Walsh, did eventually arrive.

2

The two other members of Walsh's Serious Crime team stood waiting for him by the closed steel-meshed gate.

Detective Sergeant Reginald Finch was a tall, lanky, blue-eyed man with fair hair, and in his early thirties. He was married, involved with a home for disabled children, and devoted any other spare time to an amateur interest in most things historical and archaeological.

Detective Constable Brenda Phipps was a slender, brown-eyed, very pretty young woman in her late twenties. She kept herself extremely fit and active by practising the martial arts, when she wasn't displaying an infinite patience by meticulously restoring the chipped and broken pieces of porcelain that she bought cheaply from bric-à-brac stalls and car boot sales, to add to her widely varied collection.

'The duty office says that this place is owned by a Dr Arthur King, boss,' Reginald Finch said, waving his hand vaguely towards the house from which was coming the strident ringing of an alarm bell. 'He's on Headquarters' direct call alarm system list, and the Crime Prevention section's Alert list, but he can't have lived here long, because his name's not on their copy of the electoral register yet.'

'It's a regular little Fort Knox up there, apparently, Chief,' Brenda Phipps advised, running a hand through her unruly hair. 'Automatic floodlights with video cameras on each side of the house, and the side door was reinforced with hardened steel mesh. The SOC team had a hell of a job getting in. Yes, and the overhead telephone wires have been cut.'

Walsh peered over the gate at the house. All was brightly illuminated. The Forensic team had set up portable lamps powered by the generator in a nearby white van. Its low-pitched throbbing was nearly drowned by the sound of the alarm bell.

That bell was loud enough out there where they stood – up at the house it must have been deafening.

The house was large and detached, built of red brick, with tall chimneys and a slate roof. It was set back some thirty feet from the road and fronted by a wide lawn; tussocks of grass showed above the thin layer of snow. A rose bed bordered the drive, and from the drive a path led across to the front door. There were many tracks across the lawn, some going to a lighted window; so many that Walsh feared it might be impossible to sort them all out. However, there were some clear tracks on the drive. One set were shoe prints going up, then off over to the front door; the others went to the side door and came back – those had been made by a dog. At least the Forensic team had spared those by keeping well over to the far side.

Dark figures were roaming about. A camera flashed, someone was holding a measuring frame and a tall lean figure was coming down to the gate.

'That you, Sidney?' Dr Richard Packstone said gruffly.

'Good morning, Richard,' Walsh grunted in reply.

Dr Richard Packstone was the man in charge of the Scene of Crime Forensic team. He was a widower in his early sixties, a highly experienced, taciturn man who rarely smiled, although he could be sociable enough when the need arose.

'Come in by the side gate,' Packstone invited, indicating a smaller entrance partially hidden in the tall overgrown laurel hedge. 'This big one's radio-controlled and we don't know how to open it yet. You needn't worry about all these footprints,' he went on, well aware of the other's interest in tracks and tracking. 'I've had all the approaches to the house videoed and photographed. You can study them at your leisure.'

'What have you found inside?' Walsh asked. 'Are we going to be needed?'

Packstone pulled at a stubbly chin and then adjusted his spectacles higher on the bridge of his nose. 'Speaking personally, I should think so,' he replied grimly. 'There's a prima-facie case of suicide in there, but, well, enough suspicious circumstances to warrant detailed investigation. That's why I'd rather you didn't come inside just now. We're all tripping over each other as it is. Let my lot get the preliminaries over first, but come to that front window, and see for yourselves what we're up against.'

They all stood some six feet back from the house and stared at the uncurtained window much as they might have stared at a framed illuminated painting exhibited in a picture gallery. Just as a good artist would want, the eyes of the viewers were immediately drawn to the central dramatic feature on the floor: a fully clothed man lying spread-eagled on his back. Protruding from his chest was a long bronze sword, with a blue wire-wound grip and twinkling coloured stones set jewel-like round the pommel. The face of the man could not be seen from that angle.

After an examination of that dramatic feature, the other beautifully executed details could be studied. The carved white marble fireplace, a few logs in the copper scuttle to one side of the black iron grate, a three-piece suite in soft beige leather, a low table, a book on the floor, the vague shape of things hanging on the walls, and opposite the fireplace, a closed door, varnished to highlight the grain and the lovely reddish-brown colour of old pine . . . but that fine door had been vandalized. The bottom panel had been ruthlessly cut out. Other things about the door were strange. On it was screwed a large black shed-type panel lock, and below that, a small brass bolt. Even from that distance, it could be clearly seen that the bolt was shot and closed. That was the only door to the room.

Walsh turned his attention to the window frame. It was modern, made of aluminium and holding double- or even triple-glazed panes. There were two casement windows that could open (both were in fact closed) and a centre pane, which was fixed.

'He looks dead enough, doesn't he?' Packstone commented ruthlessly. 'We had to get in quickly, just in case there was a chance that he wasn't. I didn't want to disturb the door, so I had them cut the panel out.'

Brenda Phipps voiced what was apparent to them all. 'That

man couldn't have committed suicide by falling on the sword. He wouldn't be lying like that if he had. There's not the room between the hearth and the settee for him to have turned on his back, for one thing.'

'But could a man lying in that position pull a sword that long into his own chest, by himself? Are his arms long enough, for a start?' postulated Reg Finch.

'It might be possible,' Walsh muttered doubtfully.

'We've got to wait for the pathologist to arrive before we can disturb the body, but it'll be an hour or so till he gets here. All I've done in that room so far is to make sure the man's dead,' Packstone said quietly, then hesitated as if to give more emphasis to what he was to go on to say. 'But like Reg, I doubt whether the man's arms are long enough for him to have been able to stab himself. I might be wrong, of course. In the mean time, as far as I'm concerned, the circumstances are suspicious.'

As they watched, a plastic-garbed man crawled through the hole in the bottom of the varnished pine door, followed by another. They covered the body with a clear plastic sheet, cutting a slot in the middle to allow it to pass over the sword, then they set about vacuuming the carpet near the door. Another man followed, armed with cameras.

'Good, they've done the kitchen and the hall,' Packstone went on. 'Give us another hour or so, Sidney, then you can go indoors and see for yourself. Ah! That looks like the doctor. Now we can get the man officially declared dead.'

'Those dog prints in the drive, Richard – has anyone back-tracked them?' Walsh asked. 'Whoever was walking that dog might have seen something suspicious.'

Packstone shook his head. 'I was rather more concerned with what had gone on inside the house. Those prints go right up to the side door where we went in. The dog must be a big one, it looks as though it jumped the gate down there.'

'Right! Brenda, find some torches, will you please? Then you and I can go and track the dog. Reg, you go and see this Grigson fellow, if he hasn't already gone to bed. Make sure we get to know all that he can tell us,' Walsh said emphatically.

Reg Finch turned away and winked slyly at Brenda. They both knew that the Chief Inspector loved getting on his hands and knees and doing a bit of Red-Indian tracking if he could, and such opportunities didn't come his way too often.

Mervyn Grigson's grey car still remained where he had abandoned it, its nose tucked deep in the thick hedge. It would go no further unaided. The crumpled rear wing was streaked with white and torn metal had been forced tight round the tyre. The front had probably fared even worse, although Reg Finch could not see that clearly, but the eight-inch square oak gatepost had survived intact. That had merely been pushed out of the ground, and now lay drunkenly across the drive entrance.

The Grigson house, although as secluded and in grounds as spacious and well established as its neighbour, was smaller and less modernized – it still had its original sash windows and the outside woodwork was badly in need of a coat of paint. The lights in the ground-floor rooms were still on, signifying that the owner had not yet gone to bed.

He was preparing to, though, for he was in pyjamas and dressing gown when he opened the front door to Reg's tentative knocks.

'Yes, you might just as well come in,' Grigson replied resignedly. His rather plump face seemed grey and lined, making him look much older than he probably was. 'I feel dreadful right now, I've got myself a hell of a headache. I've taken a couple of asiprins, but they haven't started to work. I couldn't sleep yet, so I was just going to have a quiet read of the papers until I feel better. I've sent the wife back to bed, there's no point in her staying up, is there? We mustn't make too much noise, though – the kids are still asleep, we don't want to wake them. Let's go in here.'

He led Finch into a comfortably furnished but very untidy sitting-room where toys, books and newspapers had overflowed from the tables and chairs on to the floor.

'Kick that stuff off,' Grigson went on, indicating a shabby

17

armchair. 'It can't make the place more of a mess than it is. Now, what do you want to know? I've already told your chaps all I can, but I suppose you want me to go through it again. Never mind. I'll start from the beginning, that's always the best place, isn't it? I sell for a London publishing firm, mostly crime and romances in hardback, that sort of thing. Been on the road with them for ten years now. Well, there's only three of us to cover the whole country. My area's eastern England and Scotland. That's where I've been all week – Scotland. They read more up there than they do down here, strangely enough. Even so, it's mostly libraries that buy our stuff, rather than bookshops. But they're all having a hard time in this recession, I can tell you. Everything's a hard sell these days. I usually try to start home after lunch on a Friday, but that didn't work out this time, so I was late getting away. Still, it was all right until I got this side of Huntingdon, then I ran into the snow and had to take things steady, but I wasn't prepared for that idiot coming hell for leather out of next-door's drive. In fact, I think I did pretty well to get as much out of his way as I did. My car'll be off the road for a fair old time, I shouldn't wonder,' he said, grimacing bitterly.

'I know it was dark, and' that the other car came straight at you with its headlights on, but did you get any idea of what make it was?' Reg Finch asked, running his long bony fingers through his fair hair, then reaching forward to move a stool to one side so that he could stretch out his legs more comfortably. Grigson's garrulity was probably one of his assets as a salesman, he could probably natter on with irrelevances until the cows came home.

Grigson puckered up his face and appeared to concentrate deeply. 'Well, you know,' he said hesitantly, 'I've been thinking about that. Funnily enough I can see the whole thing quite clearly in my mind, even though it happened so quickly. I reckon it was a Volvo. It was a bit boxy from the front, if you know what I mean, and a bit high for its width, like a Land Rover, but it wasn't a Land Rover.' He shook his head to emphasize that point. 'I also had a glimpse of it in my side mirror. It was so fleeting it's difficult to be sure, but I've the feeling it was an estate car. Square-backed with windows, so it definitely wasn't a van. No, I wouldn't put my hand on my heart and swear to it one hundred per cent, but I'm pretty sure it was a Volvo, and a white or light-coloured one at that,' Grigson went on, confidently.

Finch studied the other's face for a moment, trying to assess how accurate this piece of information might be, and concluded that the man's experience on the road had probably made him as near an expert on vehicle recognition as you were likely to get. There was a possibility of confirmation though.

'Whoever it was left streaks of paint on your back wing. An analysis of that might help,' Finch suggested. 'Now, what do you know about your neighbour, Arthur King?'

'Not a lot, I'm afraid. He hasn't been here very long. The house was empty for nigh on a year. The chap who had it before got sent to Switzerland by his firm, lucky beggar, but he had to drop the price quite a bit in the end, to get a sale. This new chap had a hell of a lot of work done on it. He moved in about a month ago, I'd say. I met him in the village last weekend, but he didn't say much about himself. Works for the university, I think.'

'There doesn't seem to have been anyone else in the house tonight. Was he married, do you know?' Reg asked.

Grigson shook his head slowly. 'That I don't know. I thought he was, to start off with. I saw a woman with a couple of young kids there while the builders were still in, but I haven't seen her since. My wife might know. You ought to have a chat with her in the morning, she usually knows what's going on around here.'

'The tracks go into the wood here,' Brenda Phipps said helpfully, flashing her torch impatiently on the other side of the lane. The Chief seemed to be spending an unnecessary amount of time studying the churned-up slush just outside the gate.

'Those are of the dog coming in,' Walsh explained shortly.

19

'It went away, yes, over there. A big dog, as Packstone said, to have cleared the gate in one jump. Come on, this way.'

The 'out' tracks also went into the wood, but a little further down the lane. The pad marks were not easy to follow. The snow under the twiggy branches of birch and elder was patchy, with plenty of bare areas, but even in those there were faint signs indented in the squelching soggy accumulations of fallen leaves. They needed searching for though, and Walsh had to bend down to peer at the ground in the light of the torches. It was also a problem avoiding unseen branches that snagged on arms and legs and threatened to poke at an unwary eye.

'Wouldn't it be better to do this in daylight?' Brenda asked in a voice totally lacking enthusiasm.

'Of course it would, but there'd be no tracks left by then,' came the grunted reply. 'The snow's melting fast. The tracks in the soft soil are all right, they'd last, but this leafy mulch stuff's like rubber, in a few hours it'll go back to how it was before. The dog limps a bit on his left side. He might have strained himself jumping that gate.'

'There's no sign of anyone being with the dog,' she protested, but merely received a grunt in reply.

Brenda sighed, and continued to follow, shining her torch as best she could to light the area in front.

The dog seemed to have wandered about aimlessly, as though it, like them, had no real idea of just where it was going, except that it had avoided any of the recognized paths and had kept to where the undergrowth was thickest.

After a while Walsh stopped and straightened his back. They were now in a small clearing, dominated by a seemingly gigantic towering oak, whose thick lower branches twisted and spread so wide and far out that it was amazing that the tree had the strength to support their weight. Brenda swung her torch round and illuminated one such branch that had given way and now rested on the ground. That tree, no doubt, was climbed by all the kids in the area in summer, and may also have been the dog's favourite, because the tracks went near the branch on the ground, then curved round, to head back the way they had come.

'Keep still,' Walsh whispered, holding up a hand. 'Listen! Someone's about. Switch off your torch.'

Without the friendly light of the torches, Brenda felt that a cold thick cloak of darkness had suddenly been drawn close around them, isolating them from the real world at their own level, while above, the twisted distorted ghostly shapes of the old oak's branches loomed ominous and threatening against the marginally lighter sky.

Brenda shivered uneasily and listened. All she could hear was a low moaning whine from the faint breeze through the bare trees. Then there came the sound of a whistle, from over to her left.

They'd need to question whoever it was, but approaching anyone in a wood in the dark was liable to be fraught with difficulty. The chances were that whoever it was would be frightened out of their wits by the sudden appearance of strangers.

'It's a bit early for anyone to be out strolling in the woods, isn't it?' Walsh whispered doubtfully.

'Too damned true,' Brenda replied, a little more emphatically than was perhaps necessary.

Walsh hesitated a moment longer, still doubtful of just how to set about things. Then he started walking forward, switched his torch on again and shouted, 'Hello there! We're police! We'd like a word with you!'

Brenda remained silent. Shielding her torch with the palm of one hand, the other raised to protect her face from the twiggy undergrowth, she ran lightly in a slightly different direction, towards where she'd thought the whistle had come from.

She heard Walsh shout again. He was making a lot of noise crashing through the bushes.

That last shout must have reached their quarry's ears, for there came a sudden high-pitched startled scream and the barking of a dog, followed, seconds later, by the cracking report of a firearm.

The sound of the shot took Walsh so completely by surprise

that he missed his footing, tripped over a branch and fell flat on his face. His torch slipped from his hand and landed some feet to one side.

He could not have followed a wiser course of action even if it had been deliberate, Walsh thought, keeping his head close to the ground, for two more shots came in rapid succession. Cautiously he tried to reach in his pocket for his radio, but he was lying on it. It would be safer for him to stay still and not move. Brenda would surely summon assistance.

Brenda did think about it, but had decided that the danger the Chief was in needed prompter action than merely crying for distant help. She had suddenly found herself on a well-trodden path, and a short distance away, outlined against the glow of light from Walsh's torch, was a dark figure with arm raised. She could deal with this situation by herself. She slipped her own torch into her pocket as she ran silently forward. Then she leapt at the unsuspecting figure, reaching out to grasp desperately at the gun-bearing wrist of that outstretched arm. She wrenched it round, fumbling to prise the fingers from the butt of the handgun, then, when she'd heard that fall harmlessly to the ground, she twisted the arm up into the small of the figure's back, in a good half-nelson.

'I've got him, Chief,' she yelled.

But she was wrong.

The figure suddenly came out of the trance brought on by the unexpected attack from behind, and Brenda found herself trying to hold a screaming, writhing hysterical female, and at the same time to deal with a yapping spaniel that had come hot-foot to the defence of its mistress and bravely tugged and growled at her ankles.

'Are you sure you're all right now?' Walsh said solicitously, when the woman had calmed down somewhat. The light of the torches revealed that she was tall, in her early fifties, and had a confident, sensible face. Not one who panicked easily, under normal circumstances, Walsh thought.

Now that her supposed assailants had been revealed as

bona-fide law enforcement officers, her attitude had become very matter-of-fact and cool.

'I'll never be all right again. My God, you did give me a fright. My heart's still going at it like the clappers,' the woman gasped out, a hand still held to her heaving chest. 'What did you think you were doing? I might have had a heart attack, then what would you have done? Left my corpse to rot in the bushes, I suppose?'

'We've already got one corpse on our hands this morning thank you,' Walsh said, pleasantly surprised to find that he, himself, had so quickly got over the unnerving shock of being suddenly fired upon. This woman seemed to have an admirable sense of humour, despite her experiences; for him to reply in the same spirit would help to normalize the situation even more. 'One's enough,' he went on, 'and it could easily have been my corpse in the bushes, not yours. Your first shot must have only missed me by a whisker.'

'You think so, do you? Well, let me tell you that if I'd aimed to hit you, I'd jolly well have hit you. My father taught me how to shoot a gun,' the woman explained proudly, as she felt in her pocket for a handkerchief to blow her nose.

Brenda raised her eyebrows at the woman's account of her marksmanship. Those service revolvers were heavy weapons, especially for a woman. To aim them with any semblance of accuracy one needed both hands tight on the grip and the right crouching stance to control the recoil. This woman had merely stuck out her arm and fired, like any pseudo-cowboy of the Wild West films. If she'd really hit what she'd aimed at, it would have been little short of a miracle.

'But', the woman went on, 'you were lucky – I wasn't using live ammunition. It was your fault anyway, startling me like that. I thought you were a rapist or some kind of homicidal maniac coming at me. What's this about another body? Is that what all the fuss down the lane is about? Someone's dead? Are you sure? Can I help? I'm a doctor.'

'Thank you, but yes and no. We have a death in suspicious circumstances, that's why we were in the wood, following tracks,' Walsh explained. 'Now, would you tell us what you are doing out at this hour, and why you were carrying this revolver? Is it licensed?'

'Good lord, I hope your dead person wasn't shot with a gun, that would be awful. Oh dear, no. I was only taking Susy here for a walk, and I carry the gun so that I can shoot any attacker, police or otherwise,' the woman explained humorously. 'No, seriously. My name is Dorothy Hammington, and I live in the bottom flat in the first house in Badon Lane. I've had a continuous string of call-outs since eight o'clock last night. Kids with tummy-aches, old people with coughs. You name it, I've had it, and I got home,' she looked at her watch, but it was too dark to see properly, 'about twenty-five minutes ago. I needed some fresh air before trying to sleep, always assuming I don't get another call-out.' She patted her pocket and half withdrew a pager. 'If this still works. As for the gun, well, I've never had to use it before, but it's not safe for women to walk about at night on their own these days, is it? It was my father's. He was an officer in the war, you know, but I only load it with blanks. As a doctor I can't go round shooting people, however much I'd like to at times, can I?'

Brenda smiled to herself in admiration of this tough woman doctor who had coped so well under such strange circumstances.

Sidney Walsh, however, frowned. He released the revolver's cylinder to allow the cartridges to fall into the palm of his hand. Three were still live, but as she had said, they were blanks, yet he could have sworn he'd heard a bullet whistle passed his ear.

'Understandable protection, Dr Hammington,' he said, shrugging his shoulders, 'but highly illegal, and if you've no licence I'm afraid I'll have to confiscate it. Did you see anyone about, a strange car parked nearby perhaps, when you went out last night?'

The woman shook her head. 'I can't say that I did.'

'What about a big dog? Did you see one of those, or know anyone around here who owns one?' Brenda asked, bending to scratch behind the ears of Susy, who had now decided to be friendly.

24

'I'm afraid not.'

'Did you know a Mr King, in the house a bit further down from yours, the one with the big steel gate?'

'No. I can't help you, I'm afraid.'

'Brenda, you escort Dr Hammington home, and take a statement listing all her call-outs last night. I'll go back and finish following those tracks. I'll see you at the scene of the other crime, in about half an hour.'

3

It was decidedly warmer now. The wind had veered round to the south-west and had brought with it a light drizzle of rain.

Dr Packstone came to the side door of the house to meet Walsh and the other two members of the Serious Crime team.

'You'll have to wear these, I'm afraid,' he said, handing over three sets of clear plastic overalls, and the washer-woman hats that would minimize the chances of their confusing Forensic by dropping any of their own hairs or other minute body traces in the house. 'You'd better take your shoes off too, Sidney. What have you been doing? You look as if you've been rolling around in a ploughed field. The pathologist will be here in about three-quarters of an hour,' he explained, talking louder than normal in order to make himself heard above the sound of the alarm bell. That continuous ringing seemed to have set the whole fabric of the building to resonate sympathetic harmonies that were increasingly maddening to minds anxious to concentrate on more important things.

'Damned noise,' Packstone muttered. 'That's the alarm control box, on the wall by the door there. I've called out the security company's agent, but I don't want to disturb anything until we know exactly what we're doing. It's a very sophisticated system, you see. There's sensors, beams and detectors all over the place. Anyway, I think we're going to be here for quite a long time. Things do not appear to be straightforward at all.' He rubbed vigorously at a lens of his horn-rimmed spectacles with a plastic-covered finger, as though some smudge was there that, like the blood on Lady Macbeth's hands, would not go away.

'In what way?' Walsh asked politely.

'Well,' Packstone replied slowly, picking his words carefully, 'that sword. I've had the hilt checked for fingerprints. It's wire-wound, which is not a good surface, but we've got a nice clear set of the right hand and part of the left, as you'd expect if the hands were overlapping. We can assume they are the dead man's, but the problem is . . .' Again he hesitated. 'They're all there is,' he went on, shrugging his shoulders. 'The sword hilt and the upper part of the blade were wiped clean before those last prints got there, and there's another obvious thing. Those prints should not be so pristine clear as they are, they should have been smudged when his hands fell away. No, suicide doesn't seem right, but I'm not making that as a positive statement yet, you understand. So that leads to the next problem. The door of that inner room, where the body is, was locked and bolted on the inside.'

'But with the house alarm set, the inner door bolted on the inside, and no one else in the room, it must be a suicide, mustn't it?' Brenda ventured.

Packstone grimaced but shook his head. 'You'd think so, wouldn't you, but, as I say, it isn't as simple as that. I wanted to give you three a chance to see things as they actually are, but I'd rather you didn't stay long, we've too much to do,' he explained.

'Was the key in the lock of that inner door? I don't remember seeing it from the window,' Walsh asked quickly.

'No, it wasn't, and that lock's another thing I don't like. It's a different type of lock than was originally fitted. It ought to be a mortice lock, inset within the door itself, but that's a shed-type panel lock that's been screwed on the inside. The keyhole on the outside of the door doesn't even line up with the keyhole in the plate of the lock, so it couldn't possibly have been locked from the outside.'

'I don't understand why the inner door needed to be locked and bolted with all this high-tech security system round the house, but if it's not suicide, then the man's killer must have gone out of the window.' Reg Finch had to shout to make himself heard above the continuous clanging of the alarm bell.

Packstone shook his head. 'That certainly didn't happen. The windows are all closed and have security locks on them. Now I know you'd like to do a search, but I'd rather that waited until we've done all the surface traces. Anyway, come on in and see the room for yourselves. You'll have to crawl through the hole in the door, but while you're in there do keep within the area of the tapes we've laid on the carpet.'

It was a brightly lit, spacious room, probably about twenty feet by fourteen or so, with the high ceiling and moulded covings much favoured by architects in the nineteenth century.

The clear plastic sheeting covering the body shimmered under the lights like a rugged block of mica-flecked grey stone, and from it, through the ·split, protruded the naked bronze sword. Had a tall begowned wizard called Merlin been standing nearby, that sword might have been awaiting a magical withdrawal – by the youthful future King of the Britons.

The man's features could not be seen clearly, but he had thick bushy eyebrows and very little signs of greying in the hair on his head. Early to middle thirties was probably a fair judgement of his age. He wore baggy brown corduroy trousers, carpet slippers and a white roll-necked sweater, now stained a darkish red round where the sword entered his chest.

The fire had long since burned out although there was still a suggestion of warmth. The ash was white and flaky from the burning of wood; there were logs in a shiny copper scuttle placed to the left of the hearth. One of the chairs of the three-piece suite had been pulled round in front of the fire, and had its back to the door. On a small polished oak table beside it were a glass containing a whisky-coloured liquid, and also a plate on which lay an unopened packet of potato crisps, a partly eaten lump of Cheddar cheese – there were teeth marks to be seen on one side – and a slice of bread, spread with what looked like butter and marmalade. There was also a flat black box with a display, rather similar to a television remote control or a pocket calculator, but larger. A hardback book lay on the floor, but Walsh could not see the title, not without stepping out of the area delimited by the tapes.

Brenda looked appreciatively round the room. The walls, although covered with an intricately embossed paper, were painted with a pale green matt emulsion, no doubt to better set off the decorative items that were hanging on them. She went over to the windows. The casement frames were holding such thick double-glazed panes that Brenda had the feeling they might be bullet-proofed. One of the stay bars for holding the window in position when open was off its peg, but as Packstone had said, all the catches were closed, and presumably locked as well. Beneath the window was a long double radiator, painted white. The curtains were thick and heavy, a lined dark green brocade that matched well with the walls, the carpet, and the colour of the three-piece suite, suggesting that someone of good taste had had a hand in their choosing. Those curtains hung from a heavy rail that combined rollers and cords so that they could be drawn together, or opened, merely by pulling the appropriate tasselled rope that hung to one side, partly obscured by the folds of material. The stitching of the lower of the two tassels had partly come away; it hung by only a few threads. A job that would take a competent woman, armed with needle and thread, only a few minutes to repair. That fact, combined with a general impression of untidiness out of keeping with the style of the room, made Brenda fairly certain that the ministrations of a woman had been lacking for quite some while. There were few ornaments, and none of the old porcelain that might have held her attention.

Reg Finch's sweeping gaze was immediately held by the sight of an ancient warrior's helmet hanging on the far wall

28

away from the window. The helmet was of a dull bronze, and set on a small, half-circular, polished oak bracket shelf. It was a replica, obviously, judging by its pristine condition. Reg racked his brains to recall where he had seen pictures of its like before. The dome of the headpiece had decorative incised lines running down from the topmost boss, and more lines emphasizing the bridge of the brow. At the back it broadened out into the shape of an eagle's tail, to protect the neck, and long curved ear-pieces hung down the sides. That, Reg finally decided, was a reconstruction of the helmet found in the Sutton Hoo Saxon prince's ship burial, although he felt sure it should, more correctly, have been made in steel rather than bronze. Below the helmet hung a circular bronze shield with a heavy central boss and with strange writhing shapes engraved on its surface. The hilt of a dagger protruded from behind the far side of the shield; the grip was wire-wound and the pommel was set with a large ruby-red stone, surrounded by smaller stones of various colours. By rights there should have been a matching weapon on the near side, to give the whole its traditional format, but that piece was missing, no doubt because it was stuck firmly in the chest of the dead man.

These things might be good replicas of actual archaeological finds, but they completely lacked any of the compelling aura that the genuine articles would possess. At least there had been no attempt to make them look old. The titles of the books in the nearby bookcase gave some explanation of the unusual wall hangings. They were mostly about King Arthur, or Britain after the Romans, or the coming of the Saxons. Some of the books themselves were old and there were a great many of them, indicative of the fascination that the romantic, mythological or perhaps legendary character of King Arthur had held in the minds and imaginations of many people for many generations. Perhaps they were, after all, very appropriate in a house owned by a man who was himself named Arthur King. A personal interest in that period, so long ago, was understandable.

Finch then turned his attention to the body on the floor. Through the plastic sheet he could see that the fingers of the hands that rested on the stomach were still half closed in a grasp that death had apparently relaxed away from the ornate hilt of the sword that had been thrust slightly upwards, between the lower ribs, to the heart. At that angle there would have been the least resistance, for ribs overlap to protect the vital organs from a downward stroke, but are open and ready to guide and route an upward thrust to its target.

It would have been no lingering death. There would have been no time to twist and writhe in final paroxysms of agony. When Finch bent closer he could see large ornate letters etched on the sword blade. 'Excalibur' were the words they formed, followed, in much smaller script, by 'Made in India'.

The bronze blade, although it had an edge of sorts, was definitely not sharp, so perhaps some power would have been needed to drive it through the thick sweater and shirt, to where it now was. The whole scene seemed too obvious and too contrived a setting to be real. It was such that a waxworks or museum might use to display some gory event as a popular tourist attraction.

Reg Finch blinked a few times and tried to concentrate harder on his observations, but it was difficult to think clearly and objectively with the constant ringing of that alarm bell jangling in his mind. In fact it was giving him a real headache. The other two gave the impression that they were impervious to those awful sounds.

He stared at the lock on the door. It looked completely wrong, there, on the varnished wooden inner door of a gentleman's elegant residence. It was more suitable for a thin board door of a garden shed or a rural cottage, and there was the little two-inch brass bolt, shot closed. Very strange. It didn't make much sense, but then nothing would, not with this incessant maddening ringing in his ears.

Enough was enough, Reg thought, there was time in plenty for going over every inch of this house – when the specialists had done their methodical work, and there was peace and blessed quiet. He crawled back through the hole in the door and went across the wide and spacious hall, observing a large, dark wood, carved chest against the far wall that looked ancient at first glance, but was probably made in

Korea, and thence made his way to the kitchen where the volume of mind-deadening sound was even greater.

Packstone was there, talking to a short freckled-faced man with thinning reddish hair.

'I just want the bell switched off,' he was saying as he pointed at the blue-painted burglar alarm control box on the kitchen wall. 'The noise is driving us all mad. You say you don't know the combination sequence?'

The other shook his head. 'No, that's always the customer's personal secret, for obvious reasons. We advise them to use the number sequence of a birthday, or something like that, so they can't easily forget it, but that's up to them. What's this powdery stuff over it? Oh! I see. You've done it for fingerprints, I suppose.'

'Of course,' Packstone replied impatiently. 'I want the computer programming left as it is, so we can record and study it. Just stop that blasted bell working.'

The other shrugged his shoulders. 'There should be a remote control box somewhere. The owner would have it with him.'

'There is, but it's in the sitting-room, where the body is. You can't have that yet.'

'Look, this system is a complicated one,' the red-haired man protested. 'That's our Fort Knox control box. The very latest crème de la crème of security systems. I'll check the manual, but I think the best I can do, if I can't have the remote control box, is to disconnect the bell from the batteries in the roof – but even that's supposed to be tamper-proof, so it isn't quite as simple as it sounds.'

'Dr Packstone,' Reg Finch interrupted, 'the car in the hedge, down the lane. There's streaks of paint on it left by the one that rammed it. Could they be analysed to identify the vehicle make, please?'

Packstone glowered at him with annoyance. 'I'll see to it, Reg,' he snapped. 'And there's some Polaroid photos of the dead man's face on the work top there. You'd better take them.'

'Thank you,' Reg said. He took off the plastic protective dungarees and went outside.

'We'll be back later, Richard. When the pathologist has been,' he heard Walsh saying behind him. Maybe the others had had enough of that noise too.

The rain had increased in intensity while they'd been within the house, and the snow had nearly all gone.

Reg looked at his watch: it was just after six o'clock. That continuous noise had made him feel physically sick. He swallowed hard. He did not want to display any weakness, not in front of all these others.

It was a great relief to hear Walsh's voice saying that they'd best get back to Headquarters, and that he'd see them both in the canteen, where they could have some coffee and breakfast.

He hurried down the lane to his car, with the tension of nausea in his stomach.

The jangling rattle of the bell still rang in his ears, long after he'd gone far enough away for the reality of it to be completely inaudible.

The Headquarters canteen was busy with shift change crews mingling noisily about the cluttered and smeared white formica-topped tables.

'She's in the corner over there, boss,' Reg Finch said, using his height to scan the room. Variations in traffic, plus the fact that she invariably drove everywhere as though she was out to achieve pole position in some international motor rally, had enabled Brenda to arrive several minutes earlier than the other two.

'I saw the duty sergeant, Chief, and told him where we'd be for a while, and the Crime Prevention sergeant is coming in to dig out his file on the dead man. I've ordered coffee, eggs, bacon and toast for you both,' Brenda announced, smiling cheerfully. 'They'll bring it over when it's ready. That's one meal you won't have to cook for yourself, Chief. How is Gwen? Did she ring last night?'

'Yes. She's in Detroit today. She says things are going very well,' Walsh replied, taking off his muddy coat and hanging it over the back of the chair. 'Now, this body in Badon Lane. It's always a mistake to start jumping to conclusions early on. It might turn out to be a suicide, in spite of what Packstone says.'

'No way, Chief,' Brenda interposed, while Reg shook his head vigorously in agreement.

Walsh seemed surprised at their reactions, and shrugged his shoulders. 'We'll see. Anyway, first things first. The dead man's next of kin – we'll need them for identification purposes.'

'Grigson said he saw a woman with young children there when the builders were in the house. He thought she was King's wife at the time, but if she was, she didn't move in with him,' Reg added.

'It shouldn't be difficult to sort that out. Obviously we've got to talk to the rest of the neighbours, they might know. You can set young Knott and Bryant on that later, Reg. Then there are the people in the car that Grigson bumped into. We must find them. He thought it was a Volvo, did he, Reg? Well, we'll act on the assumption that he's right. That car must have a badly crunched front off-side wing, so we'll warn all the local Volvo dealers and anyone who sells spare parts. They're to get the car number and let us know immediately when anyone comes in for those sorts of bits. You set that up as well, Reg,' Walsh went on. 'Now, the autopsy. Suicide or murder, that is the question. I want you both to be there.'

Reg grimaced. Standing around in a cold morgue while a body was methodically and messily dismembered was not a task he personally enjoyed at the best of times. The medical terms used were always a problem too, as well as the fact that one was supposed to make notes and ask intelligent, pertinent questions. If he felt as sick during that as the ringing alarm bell had made him feel now, a paper bag might well be a necessity, and get used. 'I'm not bothered,' was all he actually put into words.

Walsh took his elbows from the table and leaned back out of the way as one of the canteen staff came over bearing a heavy tray.

'Here you are, love,' the plump cheerful woman said, laying

33

the tray down. 'Eggs and bacon, all done with my own fair hands, and I washed them specially. That'll give you a good start to the day, that will, and keep the wolf from the door until you have your dinner. If you need more toast, just give me a shout.'

'Thank you. Very nice,' Reg said, eyeing the hard fried eggs and crispy bacon dubiously.

A short, rather stout uniformed sergeant came into the room, looked about him, then headed towards their table.

'Here's the file you wanted on Dr King, Chief Inspector,' he said. 'Let's have it back when you've finished with it. He's copped it, has he, in spite of his alarm system?'

'I'm afraid so,' Walsh replied, nodding his thanks, then he laid down his knife and fork and opened the file. 'Ah! This explains a lot,' he exclaimed after he'd read a few lines, but what it explained the other two had to wait a while to find out.

'Well, our friend Dr Arthur C. King, if that is the dead man, had a death threat made on him,' Walsh said eventually. 'He worked at a laboratory in the Science Park, where they test new drugs and medicines for the National Health Service. The death threat came from a so-called animal rights organization. That accounts for the high-tech security system in the house – it was recommended and advised by Crime Prevention.'

'Well, that gives us one place to start looking for his killer, Chief,' was Brenda's immediate comment.

'Maybe, but at least we can be a bit more positive now. Brenda, you organize setting up the files, and then start delving into whatever we have on animal rights organizations. I'll go home and change, then I'll go to this laboratory where King worked. They're sure to know about his family and whether King was married or not. If I can find the next of kin there, Brenda, I'll give you a ring – perhaps you would deal with it. I don't know when the autopsy will start, it might not be until this evening, but I'll have to see the Chief Constable first anyway. When Packstone's mob have done their stuff we'll have the chance to poke around in King's house on our own.'

'What about the dog tracks, Chief?' Brenda asked as Walsh got up and reached for his coat. 'Did you find anything?'

Walsh shook his head. 'I followed them back to where we started, and walked down the lane a bit and round the garden, but the snow had just about gone by then, so where the dog came from and went to, I don't know.' Then he reached in his coat pocket and pulled out Dr Hammington's heavy revolver. 'Oh lord, and I've still got to do something about this, and that woman who took pot shots at me.'

Brenda placed a small box on the table. 'That's the rest of her ammunition, Chief. They're all live, I'm afraid. She had no more blanks left.'

Walsh stood stock still for a moment, with a heavy frown on his face. At the time, in those woods, he'd been convinced a bullet, or something, had gone whistling past his ear. Was it possible that the woman had loaded three live and three blank rounds, and that he, Walsh, was lucky to be standing there, still alive? Surely he'd have noticed the difference when he'd unloaded the gun? He dug in his pocket for the empty cases. They had once been crimped at the end where the bullet would have been, as would be expected if they had been blanks.

Walsh picked up the box and went on his way.

Meanwhile, Reg Finch's eyes had opened wide in surprise. He'd heard nothing of guns and pot shots, so he reached out to put a restraining hand on Brenda's arm. He'd learn the full story from her when the boss was out of the way.

4

Walsh's home seemed even more lonely and cheerless than when he'd left it earlier.

He had a shower and put on clean clothes, then went downstairs to bundle all the dirty things he could find, including towels and tea cloths, into the washing machine. He'd been instructed to sort out the whites from the coloureds, but he couldn't be bothered to do that, so they all went in together. He scooped some powder into the container – he'd need to get another packet when he went shopping – and turned the programme knob. Should it be on 'A' or 'B'? He had to refer to the notes Gwen had left him. Did that stuff really need a prewash?

There was still time to put the old newspapers in the waste bin, pull out the black plastic liner, tie a big knot in the top, and take it outside for the refuse men to collect. What little washing up there was, was soon done and the kitchen left tidy.

A phone call to the garage to come and fix his car, a trip next door, to leave the ignition keys with them, and then he was ready to get on with his work.

The laboratory where Dr Arthur C. King had worked was not far from the Business and Science Park, to the north of the city.

It was so unobtrusively sited, and the position was so well obscured by the other surrounding factory units, that its existence, and its way of access, were not immediately obvious. It took some time to find.

Unlike its neighbouring buildings, the name was not advertised in large bright decorative letters. A board, only three inches by twenty, attached to the high wire fencing, sufficed. 'PZB Testing Ltd', it read.

There were two sets of steel-meshed gates. The first led to a small tarmacked parking area, and was open for Walsh to drive through. The second set was closed and consisted of a wide gate for vehicle access and another narrower one beside it, for people on foot.

A steel structure nearby held two television cameras in grey galvanized weatherproof containers, one of which moved slightly round as Walsh approached, so that it could stare at him with its large Cyclopean eye. Someone within the low, white, single-storey building beyond the wire was keeping him under close observation.

Walsh walked over to the smaller gate and took up the telephone handset.

'Detective Chief Inspector Walsh, Cambridgeshire CID, come to see Dr Parkinson,' he said, and he held up his warrant card for the camera to view. Then he wished he'd not done that, for it was an unnecessary, almost contemptuous, gesture. The camera was far too far away for the details to be clear.

As he stood there waiting, however, a strange picture came into his mind. It was as though he was standing alone on an open and exposed path to a high battlemented stone castle, with watch-towers manned by suspicious armed guards who would definitely not aim their spears and arrows to miss. He wouldn't have dared to make any contemptuous gestures then, would he? It would have been wiser to adopt a very humble attitude. The guards were probably trigger-happy, or bow-string-happy, or whatever the vogue phrase was at the time.

Those high stone ramparts may have been designed to keep people out, yet they served just as well to confine people within. High wire fences might have replaced the dyke and bailey, and cameras and sensors the high watch-tower, but those within were as well restricted and imprisoned as their predecessors had been.

So much for the passage of time, and an advanced civilization that still left so much fear for some individuals.

'Would you come up to the office, please, Chief Inspector?' came a voice from the handset's loudspeaker, and there was a clunk as a remotely controlled bolt was released in the smaller gate, which now swung open easily.

The female receptionist, in the office, gave no initial impression of being one who lived in a world of threatening fear and terror. She was a middle-aged, stoutish woman, wearing a charcoal grey jacket with over-padded shoulders, and a matching skirt that barely covered plump knees encased in well-stretched black tights. There was a suspicious, even hostile look in her brown eyes that was at variance with the welcoming smile she gave to her visitor.

'Dr Parkinson will see you in just a few minutes, Chief Inspector,' she said with a slight shake of her head. 'In the mean time, I'll make you a cup of coffee if you like. Sugar and milk?'

Dr Parkinson was a narrow-shouldered, nervous-looking man of less than average height, aged about fifty. He had a thin face, just now holding a worried expression, and a receding jaw, but his eyes, through the glass of his gold-rimmed spectacles, were bright, clear and shrewd.

'This is terrible news, Inspector,' Parkinson said expressively, his hands gripping the edge of his desk tightly. 'I've only told the senior staff so far. They are, like me, utterly devastated. You say you're treating the circumstances of Arthur's death as suspicious? That's awful. Everyone's going to be so very upset, and frightened too. As you know, some of us here have had threatening letters from misguided fanatics, because of the kind of work we do; even though we no longer use animals for testing purposes. It's all come much too close for comfort.'

'As I said on the telephone, the body has yet to be officially identified. Is that Dr King?' Walsh asked, laying one of Packstone's photographs on the desk.

'Yes! Yes, I'm afraid it is,' Parkinson confirmed. 'Now, I've got his personnel record file here. His wife, Gwenda, is his next of kin . . .'

'She wasn't in the house. Do you know where she might be?'

Parkinson pulled with difficulty at his receding chin, and twisted his mouth thoughtfully. 'Ah! Yes! Well! No, she wouldn't be. Their marriage broke up a few weeks ago. Arthur said it was because of the security system he was having fitted in his new house, but, well, we thought . . . Never mind, she left him and went back to her parents; taking the children with her, apparently.'

'Do you know where her parents live?' Walsh asked as he opened his notebook.

Parkinson shook his head. 'I don't, I'm afraid, but I can

tell you her maiden name. It's an unusual one – Killibury.'
Parkinson's fingers now drummed spasmodically on the desk
top. 'Its a once-heard never-forgotten sort of name. Killibury.
That's in Cornwall, I believe. Not far from Tintagel. I've never
been there myself, but I understand it's an ancient fort, known
as Castle Killibury – but then Arthur was mad keen on anything
to do with the old King Arthur legends. He was quite an active
member of the local Arthurian Society, you know, and even
writing a book on the subject. He'd got the notion that Camelot
was Cambridge Castle, because of the "Cam" bit. Have I got
that right, or was it another name for the earthworks out at
Wandlebury? No, I'm not really sure. He'd got so many local
place-names tied up with the legends, that I can't remember
them all. To be honest, he could become something of a bore
on the subject, so, well, we did try to avoid bringing it up as
a topic of conversation if we could. No, his wife Gwenda is a
nice sort of person, er, very pretty, but rather quiet. A peaceful
sort of person, if you know what I mean. Not really Arthur's
type. We used to gossip that he'd only married her because
of her name. Very uncharitable of us, I know, but I digress.
No, I don't know where her parents live, but it's local, I am
sure of that.'

'We'll find them,' Walsh said confidently. 'Now, his movements yesterday? Did he come to work as normal?'

'Oh yes. He put in a full day. According to the "signing-in"
book, he arrived at about half-past eight in the morning, and
went out at twelve for an hour or so to do some shopping,
then worked until sevenish in the evening. Our hours here are
variable, you see. I was here until well past eight, myself.'

'Did he say anything to you about what he planned to do for
the rest of the evening? Was he expecting visitors, for instance,
or planning to go somewhere?'

'I can't remember if he said anything, but it was his usual
night to stay in and work on his book. That does tend to
suggest that he expected to be on his own, doesn't it? He had
rather fixed habits you see, and he set aside certain evenings
for his writing.'

'I see that he'd worked here for five years, was thirty-two

years old, and had two young children, a boy and a girl, now aged two and three. I'd like a copy of this file, please, but a few more questions. What sort of character was he? Would you say he had suicidal tendencies, for instance? I'd like a detailed assessment from you in due course, but it would help if you gave me a thumbnail sketch now.'

'Well, I think you can definitely rule out the suicidal bit. He would be the last person to do such a thing. No! He was a very self-confident, imperious sort of person, with no time for any views or opinions that ran contrary to his own. He would brush those aside and completely ignore them, like, well, like water off a duck's back. He was well qualified for the kind of work we do here, and easy enough to get on with, once you knew his ways. A bit of an extrovert in some ways, yet intensely turned in on himself in others, hence the mania about King Arthur, and lately on security systems, and, well, yes, he was a bit of a ladies' man I think, even after he'd got married, but I can't give you specific proof of that.'

'You mean he played about with other women? Was that what you meant when you said that the reason Mrs King left him mightn't be as King had said – because of the security system?' Walsh asked.

'Did I say that? Well, yes, I suppose so, but the security system might well have been the straw which broke the camel's back. It was going to be awfully restrictive on her and the children, you see. My wife moans enough about the one we've got, and although it was installed by the same firm, it's nowhere near so intensive.'

Walsh nodded. 'I think I understood you to say that you test the long-term effects of drugs, medicines and pesticides here, and that although you once used live animals as, er, experimental guinea pigs, you no longer do so?'

Parkinson shrugged his narrow shoulders resignedly. 'Yes, that is so. We stopped using animals about a couple of years ago – on my insistence, I might add. We still use body tissues as a cultural medium, but we have the results of so many years of live experiments there's no real point in repeating what's already been done before.'

Walsh nodded. 'Sometime I'd like to compare the death-threat letter sent to you with the one King received, if you can find it, but right now I'd like to use your phone. Then perhaps you'd be kind enough to give me a list of all the people who work here, especially those who worked closely with King, and find me a room somewhere, where I could talk to some of them?'

'There doesn't seem much in this file on the Arthur King death-letter. Is this all there is?' Brenda Phipps asked the plump sergeant in the Crime Prevention section.

'It is as far as I'm concerned,' the sergeant replied snappily. 'The most important thing was to advise King and his family on their personal security, avoiding routine movements, bombs under cars, that sort of thing. There wasn't any point in putting a new alarm system into the house where they were living then, because they were planning to move. I gave my recommended suggestions regarding the place near Fulbourn, that's in the file, I know that.'

'Yes, that's all there. What I meant was that there's virtually nothing on the follow-up of the letter itself.'

'Oh, come off it, Brenda. What the devil do you expect? Miracles? Forensic gave the letter the twice-over, and other than the fact that it was posted in North London and had been written on a word processor, there was nothing to give any lead to the actual writer. As to whichever animal rights society it was that actually sent it, well, it doesn't say, does it? "Tried and condemned for inflicting suffering on animals and denying them their basic right to live naturally in freedom . . ." is all it says, if I remember correctly.'

'Yes, but what about the follow-up on the different animal rights organizations, local activists, that sort of thing?'

The sergeant shook his head irritably. Crime Prevention was more of public relations department really, visiting schools, advising shopkeepers and the public on security in general. There was very little in that to provoke personal stress and strain, if one didn't go out looking for trouble. Now here were the CID people nit-picking about, and a bloody woman one too who might well report him if he started cursing and swearing. Attack was the best form of defence, though. 'Why the hell should we? What would be the point? There's nothing to go on, we'd just be filling in the background for the sake of it. A waste of time. We've more than enough work in this section and few enough people to do it as it is, without making a rod for our own backs. If you want all that sort of stuff, you'll have to get it yourself, and the best of luck, too. You can start with all the undergraduates in the colleges. There's hundreds of them prepared to march up and down with a placard, shouting about all and everything and nothing. Animals, grants, old age pensions, you name it, they love it.' Attack was the best form of defence, because it worked.

'Thanks, Sergeant. You have been a great help,' Brenda Phipps said sarcastically, then tucked the file under her arm and went out and back to her own tiny office.

'Brenda?' Walsh said on the telephone. 'Apparently King and his wife had a bust-up a few weeks ago. She walked out on him and went back to mum, with the kids. Her maiden name's Killibury, spelt just as it sounds, but with two "l"s. There can't be many people with that name kicking about. I want to stay here a bit longer and talk to some of those people who worked with King, so will you follow that up and find her? Tell her we'll need her to identify the body. The duty sergeant will organize transport if necessary, and find you a policewoman to take with you.'

'Leave it to me, Chief. I'll see to it,' Brenda replied. 'By the way, one of Dr Packstone's men rang in. The pathologist arrived about an hour ago, and he reckons it'll be late afternoon before they can start the autopsy. Dr Packstone says that we can meet him at the house at two o'clock, to do a general search.'

'Fine! I'll be there. Tell Reg.'

But Brenda scowled as she put the phone down. Informing the next of kin of a sudden death was not one of the most pleasant of tasks. Seeing other people's distress, and being unable to do anything to help, never is, but in this case it was not something she could pass on to another section to do. Possibly, if this Mrs King had upped and left her husband, things wouldn't get too emotional. It was a pity to have to break off from this animal rights business, though. In the initial stages of an inquiry there were always many leads that needed following up, all at the same time, but it was also a danger period, for if one rushed about, trying to do too much too quickly, the chances were that nothing would be done properly, then most of it would have to be done again.

There were only two Killibury names in the telephone directory, both males. She made a note of the addresses. It would have been quicker just to have dialled the numbers but that was not an acceptable way of dealing with this problem.

Brenda picked up her fur-collared suede coat, and went out of the office and down to see the duty sergeant in the front office, still thinking about animal rights organizations. If there was no dossier kept locally, then it might well be worth getting in touch with other constabularies, particularly the Met, before tackling the problem head on. She could start interviewing activists herself, if she could find any, but the chances of getting ready co-operation from them, even with a murder involved, were probably not high.

'This is the area I want you to cover,' Reg Finch said, pointing with a long bony finger to the large-scale map that was folded so that the Fulbourn district was uppermost. 'This is Badon Lane. It goes out from the village in this north-easterly direction, towards the old Saxon fortified lines at Fleam Dyke and the Devil's Dyke, and crosses the ancient prehistoric trackway, the Icknield Way, out there on the chalk ridge that runs towards Newmarket and thence on to the north Norfolk coast.'

The duty office had collected eight junior uniformed officers for the task of house-to-house inquiries.

'Now, you've all done this sort of thing before. Ask your questions clearly. Make sure they understand what you're saying, and don't put words into their mouths for them. I won't go through the list of questions again, but vehicle movements are very important, particularly white Volvo estates. Yes, and big dogs, colour and breed unknown. Any questions? No? Right, Detective Constable Bryant will be in charge. Any problems, see him. You know where to go. On your way then. Not you, Alison, there's another job I'd like you to do for me.'

'I'll phrase the question, "any Volvo part appertaining to the front off-side," Reg,' Detective Constable Alison Knott said, her plump face creased in a ready smile.

'Yes, that'll do fine, as long as they know what "appertaining" means.'

'We've got all the garages, spare parts and breakers' yards on the computer. It won't take long to set this all up. Anyone buying a Volvo front off-side part will be recorded, as from about an hour's time. You said you would be attending this Mr King's autopsy, didn't you? I don't want to be pushy, but is there any chance I could come along too? I've done my traffic accident bit in training, of course, and blood doesn't worry me, but I've not done a real live murder autopsy,' she explained tentatively.

'"Real live" is hardly the right way to describe an autopsy, Alison, but I don't see why not. Mind you, I don't know for sure when it will start. These Home Office pathologists are kept pretty busy. They're aren't many of them about, you see. Yes, you can come by all means. It'll be good experience, but until then there's plenty for you to get on with, what with this Volvo business and the other cases we're working on,' Reg Finch replied.

Alison nodded happily. She hadn't been in Chief Inspector Walsh's section for very long, but she had soon learned that if one worked hard and did one's best, then, well, it was like a big happy family, and far far better than walking the beat, standing around at football matches or working in the front office, which were the lot of many young policewomen.

5

The rain had stopped, but the dark hurrying clouds threatened more to follow.

Brenda Phipps drew up outside a pebble-dashed semi-detached house on an estate not far from Addenbrooke's Hospital. This was the first of the two Killibury addresses. A small Panda car pulled in behind her.

The style of the house and the generously sized plots suggested that it, and its neighbours, had probably been built in the 1930s for letting by the council. Now many of them were privately owned, judging by the new-looking varnished oak front doors, aluminium-framed replacement windows and solidly built garages.

There were no such signs of affluence with this one though. The curtains in the front downstairs room were still drawn and there was a general air of untidiness. An ancient rickety wooden shed stood at the end of a long weedy shingle drive, on which were three cars. The first, nearest the road, was a nearly new Rover Metro, the second was an old grey Cortina with the bonnet up, and the third, also a Cortina, was stranded wheel-less, propped up on bricks.

Brenda got out of her car, signed to the young policewoman in the Panda to stay where she was, then headed down the crumbling tarmac path to the front door. However, when she saw that there was someone working at the far side of the Cortina with the bonnet up, she changed direction, and went over there instead.

'Mr Killibury?' she asked quietly of the man who was bending over and reaching down in the engine compartment.

Perhaps the man was of a naturally nervous disposition, for the sound of her voice made him suddenly straighten up in alarm, and in doing so his arm dislodged the bonnet staybar. Brenda's arm stopped the bonnet's downward progress in time to prevent any injury.

'What the hell did you have to creep up on me for?' he protested breathlessly. He was a short, thin-faced man who would probably have looked weedy, had it not been for the thick, stained, parka that he wore. His pale blue eyes looked accusingly at his visitor, and his greasy hands came up to press on his upper chest, where, presumably, he thought his heart might be. 'Shocks like that ain't good for me ticker,' he went on.

'I'm sorry I startled you, but you were so absorbed in what-ever you were doing that you didn't hear me,' Brenda replied pleasantly.

'I can't get the blasted nut loose. Some beggar's used the wrong-sized spanner, now it's gone all round and manky. I can't get a grip on it, no how.'

'Are you Mr Killibury? I'm looking for a Mrs King. Is she your daughter?' Brenda asked.

The man nodded towards the house. 'She's in there. Don't ring the front door bell, you'll wake mum. Go round the back.'

'I'm Detective Constable Phipps, Cambridgeshire CID,' Brenda announced, drawing her warrant card from a pocket in her suede coat and holding it out for him to see. Her hand had a line of greasy dirt across the palm from contact with the car's bonnet. She rubbed at it with the cleanest of the rags available, but that still left a mark that only soap and water would eradicate. 'I've some bad news for her, I'm afraid. Is there somewhere I can talk to her on her own, or with your wife present, perhaps?'

'That bugger of a husband wants her car back, I suppose, or is he trying to take the kids off her?' Mr Killibury's face held an expression of angry concern in place of what was probably the usual one of bovine amiability.

Brenda shook her head. 'We think her husband is dead. Is that him, on this photograph?' she said bluntly.

46

The other's face now showed bewildered shock, mixed with distress. 'Oh lord!' he said, nodding his head slowly. 'If it ain't one thing it's another. That ain't going ter go down well, I can tell you. Best come round the back.'

There was washing on a line down the middle of the garden, and an oniony smell of cooking came from a half-open, steamed-up kitchen window.

'Jenny, come out here a minute, will you? It's important. I need you,' he yelled through the window.

Jenny was presumably his wife, and a few moments later a frowning plump fair-haired woman with a blue apron over her grey dress came hurrying out of the back door.

'What do you want? What's the matter now?' she said impatiently, then stopped short when she saw a stranger with her husband.

'Jenny, this here girl's a police officer come to tell Gwenda that Arthur's dead. She's got this photo of him too. You'd better deal with it,' he suggested hopefully.

'Blimey, that's him all right. Not that we ever saw him come round here, we weren't good enough for the stuck-up prig,' she responded, rubbing anxiously at her nose, obviously thinking hard. 'We'd better get the kids out of the way first. Just give me a minute to get their coats on, Bert, and then you can take them down the road to the shop in the push-chair, buy them some sweets or something.'

'I'm sorry to have to tell you, Mrs King, that a man was found dead in your husband's house, early this morning. We believe it to be your husband, but we need to have the body formally identified,' Brenda said hesitantly, watching the blandly pretty face of the deceased man's wife suddenly became distressingly horror-struck.

The wide, deep blue eyes moistened into tears. 'But, it can't be. It can't be true,' came the words.

'I'm sorry,' Brenda repeated lamely.

Mrs King blinked several times, put her hand to her mouth,

then ran out of the room. The noise of her feet as she went up the stairs could not drown out the sounds of uncontrolled sobbing.

'I'm sorry,' Brenda said yet again. 'If there's anything we can do.'

Mrs King's mother looked at her blankly, but shook her head resolutely. Family grief was a family matter, and those who cared would rise to the occasion as countless of generations had done before them. Already the mother's jaw was hardening, preparing to take the strain, to suffer what had to be suffered for those she loved. 'Leave it to me. I'll go up to her in a minute. She's taken it bad. I thought she would. He was a swine, but that don't make it any easier for her. What happened to him, anyway? An accident?'

'We won't know for certain until after the autopsy, but we'll need to talk to her, when she's identified the body. I can organize transport for you both, if you want to go with her, and I've a policewoman outside who can stay and look after the children,' Brenda went on.

Mrs Killibury nodded. 'That's a good idea. Yes, send her in. It'll take a bit of time for it all to sink in, but Gwenda'll get over it, in time. I'll go up to her shortly.'

Brenda had wanted to ask where Mrs King had been the previous evening, whether she had gone out alone for long enough for her to go the short distance to Fulbourn, kill her husband, then return. An obvious and necessary set of questions, but the posing of them now would be callously inconsiderate. They would have to wait.

The Chief Constable was reading one of the many files piled high on his desk as Walsh came into his spacious office. He looked up, nodded his large balding head and waved a hand vaguely towards a chair and a coffee pot standing on a nearby low table. 'Sit down, and fix yourself a cup. Let me finish this first,' he grunted.

Walsh eyed the shiny silver pot warily. He'd drunk a lot of coffee already that morning, so he left it alone. He wasn't offended or surprised by the big, burly red-faced Chief Constable wanting to finish what he was reading. Sitting as that man did, on the administrative top of a mighty pyramid, responsible for the activities of several hundred police officers, as well as a multi-million pound budget, paperwork inevitably took up the bulk of his extensive working day. Assistants he had in plenty and much of his responsibility he could delegate, but reading reports and files was the only real way he could keep in touch with what was actually going on at ground level, where his force interfaced with the public that they were there to serve. His time had to be carefully shared out between the sections of his constabulary, and meetings were scheduled several days ahead; but some people, like Walsh, had direct access to him at any time of the day or night. For serious crime followed no set routine or pattern; furthermore, it could have equally serious publicity and public relations implications. It was therefore something he wanted to know about immediately, and that meant direct verbal communication rather than written reports.

Walsh looked round the familiar room with its dark brown cord carpet, oak-panelled walls and coved artexed ceiling, a mish-mash of decorative effects in a relatively modern building. They weren't solid oak panels anyway, they were eight by four sheets of oak-faced plywood, with mitred beading nailed on in squares to give the right effect. On them, evenly spaced out, were half a dozen copies of Stubbs's horse paintings, in plain wooden frames. The addition of a few horse brasses, warming pans, faked crossed swords and warriors' helmets, Walsh thought, would complete the tasteful décor – of an ultra-modern public house saloon bar.

'Right,' the CC said eventually. 'What's up? A middle of the night job, I believe.'

Walsh nodded, and briefly explained the nocturnal adventures of the salesman, Grigson, that had resulted in the mobilization of so many people.

'This death threat the dead man had was from an animal rights organization, was it? How did they take the news where he worked?'

49

'They were pretty blasé about it, really, whatever they actually said. The one that seemed to take it worst, now I come to think about it, was the receptionist. When I left she looked as white as a sheet.'

'Which animal rights organization was it?'

'The letter doesn't say. It wouldn't be one of the main ones, they wouldn't get involved in anything like that.'

The CC nodded his head and drummed his fingers on the desk. 'It's an emotional subject, animal rights, but some anarchist groups latch on to that sort of thing, just to create trouble. Mind you, it's the kind of half serious and half rag-day thing a few hot-head undergrads might get up to. It might pay you to have a word with that old professor at Downing. He usually knows what's going on in the university. He might give you a lead.'

'He might, but we'll be after extremists who are prepared to use violence. Perhaps the anti-terrorist people in London keep tabs on such people.'

'They might tell us if the request comes from a high enough level. Leave that to me. I'll see to it. This room was locked and bolted, you say, and the alarm system was working? Why are you so damned sure this King fellow didn't commit suicide? He could have fallen on his sword, couldn't he? It was a historically popular method once, until revolvers came along, not that I'd fancy either myself, but it would account for the clear set of prints. All he needed to do was hold the sword in the right position as he fell forward. I don't see the need for all this fuss.'

Walsh shook his head. 'There's not the room, for one thing. He lay in the middle of an area between the hearth and the settee. To end up on his back as he did, he would have needed to fall on the sword either in the fireplace itself or on the settee, which doesn't make a lot of sense. And why wipe the sword clean of prints before he did it? He's hardly likely to be worried about getting infected by germs, is he?' Walsh replied shortly.

The CC fingered his fleshy chin as he stared remorselessly back at Walsh, unmoved by the sarcasm. 'What does

Packstone think? He hasn't rung me yet. What's he up to?'

'He thinks as we do, that the circumstances are more than just highly suspicious. He's got everyone there going through the place with a fine-tooth comb.'

A deep frown appeared on the CC's broad forehead. 'And no doubt spending a bloody fortune on overtime and lab costs. None of you lot seem to care a damn about keeping within your financial budgets,' he growled. 'I'd like to be a bit more certain that this ain't a suicide before we go too bloody mad. Let me know the pathologist's opinion as soon as it's available. At least I know he's got his head screwed on right.'

The PXB Testing senior employees' dining-room was small, and sparsely furnished. Other than the long deal table and six chairs, it only contained a low narrow sideboard, on which stood some glasses, a carafe, a few sherry bottles, and a plant pot holding a small flowering Busy Lizzie.

'We've really got to do something. Else they'll pick us off one by one,' Dr John Bailey announced, striking his fist energetically and unnecessarily hard on the table, setting the wooden pepper pot wobbling precariously.

The four others there looked sceptically at the youngest of them all, with expressions varying from supercilious aloofness to downright contempt for the silly, ill-considered utterances of youth.

'Such as what?' Dr Parkinson, the executive director, demanded from the head of the table

'Well, we can't just do nothing,' Bailey explained emphatically.

'That's a double negative statement which merely repeats, but adds nothing to what you've just said,' Dr Anita Grant said, tempering the reproof in her words with a slight smile.

She looked momentarily at the vacant place at the table where Arthur would normally have sat, and found herself extremely pleased that his death had left her so emotionally undisturbed. That showed the wisdom of not getting too involved in relationships with men. In her younger days, and that was not so very long ago, she had revelled in the attention men had given her. It had taken time and some heart-breaks for her to realize that most, if not all, had been merely using her for their own sexual gratification. Her mother had found that lesson out the hard way too, with three husbands and a string of lovers, all of whom had discarded her when she'd served their purpose.

So, Anita Grant had formulated a different attitude. She now used men to satisfy her sexual needs – when she chose. The ever-willing, so proud of himself Arthur King, had been an ideal stud to call on, until his wife had left him. Since then, though, Anita had found that he'd thought he could have her whenever he wanted. But, oh no, no! That was how her father had used her mother, and it wasn't going to happen to her like that. However, now that Arthur was out of the way permanently, a replacement was going to be needed, and John Bailey was a possibility, even if he was five years younger than she was. He'd got his degree, somehow, but he was rather childish in some of the things he said and did – still, he was tall and fit, and had rather nice eyes.

'Pass the ketchup, please, Graham,' Anita Grant went on to ask.

'Lord! I really don't see why anyone puts half-decent food in front of you, Nita, when you insist on smothering it all over with that muck,' Dr Graham Peters voiced in disgust as he handed the bottle over.

Anita stared at him and raised one eyebrow with the practised expression of astonishment usually reserved for those occasions when one viewed the pallid and bleached creatures exposed by the lifting of a stone. 'Where matters of good taste are concerned I don't think you've any case to make, Graham. That ghastly jacket you wear all the time is offensive to the discerning eye. It might suit a bookie's runner of the fifties vintage, but I doubt it. In any case, why be unkind to bookies' runners, I say?' Anita's right eyelid closed in a wink aimed for John's benefit; she was rewarded in return with an appreciative grin that really was quite attractive.

'Please, do show some respect for our departed colleague,' Dr Parkinson protested, holding up his right hand.

'Come off it, Neil. If there are such things as heaven and hell then he must already be lining up with his coal shovel,' Dr Peters suggested, his lean features twisted into a sneer.

'No way, he's probably buttering up his beloved King Arthur, offering to clean his harp in exchange for a seat at the Round Table with all the other fanatics,' the grey-bearded Dr Jim Moflat chuckled.

'He won't have time for that, not with all those lovely angels up there dressed in those filmy see-through gowns. He'll go barmy if he doesn't get his hands up those two or three times a day. I fully anticipate the numbers of fallen angels to increase dramatically from now on,' Dr Peters guffawed.

'Decency and good taste seem noticeably lacking in the older generation, wouldn't you agree, John?' Anita Grant said cuttingly, but giving him another wink.

'I'd rather you expounded on the point you were making earlier, John. What do you suggest that we do?' Neil Parkinson inquired, anxious to change the subject. It wasn't the needling sarcasm itself that upset him – that was unfortunately the norm in this place.

'These animal rights activists, they're like the IRA,' John Bailey explained enthusiastically. 'They carry out atrocities like this and think they can get away with them because their victims still abide by the law. I was merely saying that we ought to do something to retaliate in some way – make them suffer some of the treatment they dish out.'

'If that's saying we ought to form the equivalent of a Loyalist group and go round murdering them as well, then I think you've got your values mixed up. We'd be no better than they are,' Graham Peters pointed out.

'I've a lot of sympathy for the views of the animal rights movements, myself. I cannot condone cruelty, whatever form it takes,' Jim Moflat announced.

'Neither do any of us, but you haven't had a death threat made at you, Jim. You might think otherwise if you had,' Anita said firmly. 'But I don't think John was suggesting retaliation in kind, were you?'

'But it's not for us to do anything at all. It's a matter for the police,' Neil Parkinson interrupted. 'If doing something means helping them to find Arthur's killer, then I wholeheartedly concur. I've made up my mind to give that inspector the file we've built up with all the activist names we know, and I'll speak to the chairman of the Medical Testing Association, to ask for all the help and information the other members might have accumulated. That's being positive, isn't it?'

'I was too young for the last world war, thankfully,' Jim Moflat mused absentmindedly, having lost the drift of the conversation. 'And now I'm too old, in my opinion. If you want to start taking pot shots at innocent people, John, who are just a little over-enthusiastic in a genuine cause, then count me out. On the other hand, if you can point a finger at anyone who kills in cold blood, well and good, but let the law handle it.'

'It's all very well to say that, but this killing of Arthur may encourge others to go just that extra step further than they've been prepared to go until now. I think we're all in danger. We've all got to be that much more careful,' Anita warned.

Neil Parkinson nodded. 'Yes, I do agree with that, and I've warned our security staff to be extra vigilant, but do remember that the police have no idea yet who killed Arthur. Now, I think we all ought to get back to work and try not to dwell on this problem too much. Anyone who wishes to pay their last respects at Arthur's funeral, whenever it is, may of course do so. That's the least we can do.'

'John,' Anita said thoughtfully, when they met in the corridor later, 'I've been thinking about what you were saying earlier, about us actually doing something. It's no good expecting help from people like Jim and Graham, they're too old and set in their ways, but I think we ought to talk it through at least — if you're serious, that is?'

'Oh yes, I'm serious right enough,' John replied determinedly.

'Well then, why not pop round one evening, when you've done your rowing or squash or whatever it is you do. Maybe we can work something out.'

John looked speculatively at Anita's attractive face. Invitations to pop round to a single woman's place invariably meant that there were ulterior motives in the offing. Was this a challenge to his virility? Was this an invitation saying that if he was a real man he'd come, but he was a mouse if he didn't? Either way, it was the kind of challenge that he could not pass up.

'Not tonight,' he replied quickly, licking his lips. 'I've a squash match in Newmarket that'll go on too late, but I can manage tomorrow. If that's all right?'

'Fine, come about nineish. That'll be fine.'

6

It was shortly after two that afternoon when Reg Finch arrived back at the house in Badon Lane.

The last of the snow had gone; now it was mild and there was even a drying breeze.

As he walked up the drive, nodding as he passed the uniformed constable stationed there to deter unwanted visitors, the alarm bell started its resonating, mind-penetrating ringing, but only for a few seconds, for it then stopped abruptly.

The kitchen was crowded.

Walsh, Brenda and Packstone were watching three others, two of whom were the Forensic department's systems and computer experts; the third was the short freckle-faced man who had been there earlier in the day, and who was, Reg supposed, the security company's alarm engineer. On the work units were spread a number of blueprint-sized layout drawings.

'You'd better come through into the dining-room,' Dr Packstone suggested, the unaccustomed frown now seemingly etched permanently on his brow. 'The fingerprinting, the video and still photography are all done, as well as the floor-vacuuming downstairs, but they're still doing the bedrooms.'

The vacuuming referred to the use of a small but powerful cleaner to suck up the surface debris from specified areas, into little plastic bags. The analysis of that material in the laboratory, be it skin particles, wool fibres or plain mud, might later provide the evidence to prove that a certain individual had been in that house at some time, provided, of course, that the CID could find that certain individual.

'What we're doing now,' Packstone went on, 'is to check out the alarm system in detail. There must be a hole in it somewhere.'

'What did the pathologist have to say, Richard?' Walsh asked.

'He agrees with me, he's ninty-nine per cent certain that the man didn't commit suicide. As we thought, the dead man's arms just aren't long enough,' he explained. 'His fingers could grip the sword hilt, we knew that from the fingerprints, but that was only with his shoulders hunched and his arms at full stretch. When we withdrew the sword to where it must have been before it entered the chest cavity, his fingers couldn't reach far enough to make the form of grip his fingerprints indicated. Those few inches make all the difference.'

'And the one per cent doubt?' inquired Brenda.

'Prudence, Brenda. At this stage it would be foolish to be too dogmatic. There are many things we don't yet know. There might be an explanation for what we think is unexplainable.'

'I still don't see why the sword was wiped clean before it was used,' Reg said. 'Unless the killer handled it without gloves. Very careless of him if he did.'

'We've plenty of prints round the place. Some of them have yet to be identified,' Packstone replied.

'But effectively we do have a murdered man in an enclosed

room, locked and bolted on the inside. Have you found a key to that odd lock on the door?' Walsh asked.

'Yes, the key's on the man's key-ring, and that was in his pocket, but that locked room is not the only problem. That room is within a house guarded by a highly sophisticated alarm system; one that so far appears to be all-embracing and also fully operational. They're doing a second test run now.'

'It's like one of those eggs within an egg, Chief,' Brenda proposed. 'The inner one is the locked room, the middle, the alarm system, and the third, a fall of snow. The only tracks, other than those of the dog that wandered through the wood, go to the front windows, which were locked and couldn't have been used as an entrance – oh yes, and those of that chap Grigson, which go to the front door.'

'Set out for us the basic principles of the alarm system, would you, Richard? Just how sophisticated is it?' Sidney Walsh asked calmly.

Packstone's fingers drummed lightly on the reproduction antique mahogany dining-table. 'Very sophisticated indeed, for a small private house. The system is really designed, I understand, for big multi-room places with valuable contents, such as art galleries, museums and big office blocks, but it's very adaptable. Here there are really two systems, combined into the one control panel. The garage is alarmed, you see, to protect the cars. That's linked with the automatically opening front gates and garage doors. They're activated by remote control from inside the car or by the use of a handset. When the owner comes down the road and presses his button, the gates will only open if the garage area is secure. If it's night-time, then the floodlights come on so that he can see for himself that there's no one lurking around. There are electronic sensors to warn him if anyone approaches when he goes from the garage to the side door of the house, and the video camera on that wall records it all. That's all right, no problem there, but the house system works independently. That's designed to warn of an entry any-where, authorized or not, regardless of whether the owner is at home or not.'

57

'So the system is on all the time, effectively?' Reg Finch asked, wincing slightly as the bell rang out again for a few moments.

'Effectively, yes. If the house is unoccupied and an unauthorized intruder is detected, the warning is transmitted through a radio telephone link to the owner of the house. If the owner doesn't authorize the entry within a few minutes, then the system automatically rings the police station,' Packstone explained.

'So, if whoever cut those overhead telephone wires was planning to break in, the alarm would have been activated?' Brenda interrupted.

'Yes, that's right. Those cut wires are the normal telephone wires, nothing to do with the alarm,' Packstone answered. 'Now, where was I? Yes, if the owner is within the house, as he was last night, then a warning signal is fed to a portable control box that the owner has with him all the time. Again, if the owner doesn't acknowledge that warning within a certain time, the system rings the police. Anyone approaching the house, whether it's the postman coming to the front door, or the owner coming home from work, activates the outside floodlights and video system, and all is recorded and timed. We know from those tapes that the owner came home last night at seven thirty-five and that it was snowing at the time. After that, until we arrived, the only people recorded are the two characters who presumably cut the telephone line, and Grigson, the salesman fellow from next door. I'll have copies of the video cassettes made for you as soon as I get time, so you'll be able to see for yourselves.'

Walsh nodded. 'Please! If it shows the two characters it might be a great help in finding them.'

'It might,' Packstone continued, frowning at having his line of thought interrupted again. 'Well, we're checking every outside door or window again, with everything fully operational. The owner was here, alone, last night, according to the system – yes, that's where I'd got to, the internal operation. The owner carries a master portable control box – you probably saw it on the table in the room where the body was. Anyone else has to carry a smaller unit with them, so that the sensors in each room recognize them as legitimate occupants, and don't trigger the alarm when they move from room to room, but there wasn't any other occupant last night: if the owner knows that he's alone in the house he can set his control box so that only he has free movement, and that's how we have found the master control set, and, as I say, that master control box was in the locked and bolted room with the body. So even if anyone had managed to get in undetected and had concealed himself somewhere in the house, he wouldn't have been able to move about, not without setting the system off.'

Walsh frowned and pulled at his left ear. 'Let me get this straight. Are you saying that there are sensors in each room to warn if any unauthorized person just moves about, let alone sensors on every point of entry, doors or windows upstairs and downstairs, to detect anyone coming in that way or even approaching the house too closely?' he asked.

'Yes!' Packstone confirmed. 'Each room, and that includes passages, landings, stairs, hallways, bathrooms and toilets, all have heat, smoke and vibration detectors as well as electronic beams. Every outside door and window, including those upstairs, have mechanical locking devices, all of which are undisturbed and in place, as well as electronic contacts wired up to the main system; and every single damned thing works perfectly,' he said, shaking his head bemusedly. 'It's all been checked at least once, each contact, each sensor. They're doing it now for the second time, and they'll have to keep on checking until they do find something wrong. Somehow or other someone must have come in and gone out.' Packstone's face showed a rather wild sense of bewildered determination.

'If, just supposing,' Brenda asked doubtfully, 'the dead man brought a visitor in with him who didn't wander about, could that person have got out of the house without setting the alarm off?'

Packstone shook his head emphatically. 'No! But I told you he was alone on the video when he came home, and with the master box set on lone occupancy, as it was, the alarm would certainly have gone off. We've tried that three times so far.'

'There's only one master control box in the house at the

moment, presumably, but what if someone was already in the house with a duplicate of that control box? Someone perhaps who had a similar system installed in their own house? What then?' Walsh wanted to know.

'We've thought of that, but we haven't got hold of a duplicate to try yet,' Packstone admitted. 'But the security company's handbook states that the system is programmed to accept only one master bleeper at any one time. There can be any number of subsidiary bleepers of course, but what that actually means in practice we'll find out later. The snag with those questions is that the system should still have recorded anyone going out, even if they had the right door key.'

'Lord! Living here must be like living in a prison,' Brenda said scornfully. 'Maybe it wouldn't be so bad for someone on their own, but this King had a wife and kids, or he did until she walked out on him. Now I can understand her doing that, with all this going on. Just think what it must have been like for her. Wearing bleepers about the house all the time. Whatever next? Did her kids have to have bleepers on their pyjamas when they were in bed, just in case they went to the bathroom or into mum's bedroom for a cuddle? And what about visitors, for heaven's sake? What if she wanted to take the kids for a walk or pop up to the local shop? Did she have to go through all that rigmarole of going in and out? What about the summer-time, when they'd have the doors and windows open and want to play in the garden?'

Packstone shrugged his shoulders. 'I don't know, Brenda, but it doesn't affect the situation here now, does it? You must remember that our own crime prevention advice emphasized the vulnerability of his wife and children to the threat of hostage-taking or kidnap, Brenda. The man had had a death threat, which was taken seriously; rightly so, as it turns out. That puts a strain on everyone in his family,' Packstone said emphatically, obviously not feeling happy about being put under pressure to explain the illogical results of logical reasoning. 'You can see, though, what I meant when I said the system was really designed for a much bigger multi-roomed place, with guards. One guard would stay in the guard-room with the master control, then the other guards with the smaller units could patrol the building, going from room to room without setting off any of the detection sensors. The master control would know exactly where they were too, all the time. That's why there's a computer in this system, there are so many permutations of activity.'

'Had the control box been tampered with, Mr Packstone?' Brenda wanted to know.

'Not according to the man who installed it. In any case, the program can't be got at, not without setting the alarm off.'

'The lock on the side door, is there any sign that that's been played about with?' Reg asked.

'It's a seven-lever contact-maker. It looks all right, but we'll have it stripped down later.'

'What would have happened to the alarm system if the mains electricity was switched off?' Walsh inquired.

'Nothing, at least for a while. Power cuts are to be expected occasionally and the system is designed to cope. The control box has built-in rechargeable batteries powerful enough to maintain the circuits and programs for quite a long time, rather like those modern electronic central-heating programmers. The batteries for the bell are much bigger, of course, and are in a secure container up in the roof space.' Packstone sighed and looked even more depressed.

'We'll have to leave the technical side to you and your experts, Richard. You'll sort it all out eventually,' Walsh said encouragingly. 'We'll just browse about. His personal papers might contain something to shed a light on our darkness.'

'Go ahead, there's some in the bureau in the sitting-room, and more in a drawer in his bedroom, upstairs. The post-mortem is scheduled to start at about five thirty, Sidney, so I suggest we leave here by quarter-past, it's not far. Hopefully we might get the external examination of the body done tonight. I don't particularly want to work late, I feel tired enough as it is,' Packstone mumbled as he left to go back to the kitchen.

There was no need to crawl through the hole in the bottom panel since the door was now open. The bolt and lock had been removed, and so had the body.

Before he went into the room Reg Finch lifted the lid of the carved wooden chest in the hall. It was empty, and it was a reasonably well-made modern replica, from Turkey.

Walsh went to kneel down by the white marble fireplace. He twisted his head round as he leaned forward on his hands, so that he could peer upwards past the fireclay lining to where the Victorian or possibly even Georgian brickwork showed. It was no casual interest this, apparently, for he pushed himself up from his knees and went out to find a torch, then he was back to that awkward neck-twisting position, and peering up into the gloomy darkness. That chimney had been swept recently – thicker deposits of soot occurred mainly in the corners of the nine-inch square aperture and along the mortar coursing where the rougher surface had enabled it to maintain a firm enough grip to resist the chimney-sweep's brushes. Elsewhere, though, the deposit was light and even, soft and almost woolly and containing, in places, a few flakes of the white wood ash that had been drawn upwards from the hearth by the chimney's draught.

Brenda Phipps also ignored the bureau. She went over to the window where the stay-bar had previously been disturbed. Now it was back in place. The locking mechanism on the catch lever was operated simply by a square tapered tommy bar. She used a knuckle to press round the glass and the frame, but all seemed sound and solid. Then she pulled on the shorter of the curtain cords and observed those curtains being drawn smoothly and easily across the window, to meet neatly in the middle leaving no gap.

'Do you mind, Brenda?' Reg Finch's voice protested from where he now knelt by the bottom drawer of the bureau, which he'd taken right out.

'Sorry,' she replied, and pulled the other cord, returning the curtains to their original positions. Then, in order to inspect the window's hinges, she moved the catch, and pushed it open. The alarm bell immediately started its clamorous ringing, followed by some exasperated shouts from the kitchen. Brenda quickly shut the window and turned to face the angry-looking Packstone who had appeared at the door.

'I'm sorry,' she uttered, interrupting his exclamation of 'For Pete's sake! What the devil —'

'Give me a hand over here, Brenda. I haven't got to do all this on my own, have I?' Reg Finch called out.

'Right, yes,' she said and, looking rather chastened, went over to join him.

Packstone went out muttering to himself.

'He'd got ten thousand in the building society, boss, five thousand in a special deposit high interest account, and was two hundred overdrawn on his current account,' Reg announced.

'And he'd got shares in British Telecom, British Gas, Anglian Water, Sainsbury's and a whole load more. This lot could add up to a fair old sum,' Brenda exclaimed, now with a file in her hands and the second of the drawers beside her.

'Aha,' Walsh uttered non-committally, while thoughtfully judging the weight of a heavy iron poker in his hand and studying the large knobbed end. He put it down, wiped the dust from his hands on his handkerchief, and went to study the replica of the ancient shield on the wall opposite the window. The handle of the dagger protruding from behind the shield was slightly smaller than that of the sword, but otherwise it matched. The large red pommel stone was multifaceted glass and bigger than any genuine ruby ever found. It drew out of its holder without difficulty, and so, probably, would have the missing sword, Walsh decided, when he had removed the shield. He had been hoping to find a complicated clip or restraining wire preventing its easy removal, which might have necessitated a glove being removed to free it, and hence, the wiping of the handle free from fingerprints – a point that was still puzzling him; but there was no explanation there.

Then he went upstairs to read through the deceased's personal and private papers, until Packstone came up to say it was time to go to the autopsy.

'I've got an address book, boss. There's a sister living in Norfolk, and lots of handwritten pages in a file, which are probably the book he was working on,' Reg said.

'There's a load of letters I've still to go through. Some are from friends, but most are to do with an Arthurian Society, Chief,' Brenda added.

'Right, and I've got some old papers from his university days, though I don't think they'll be of much use. Come on, let's get to this autopsy,' Walsh instructed.

'You don't really need me there, do you?' Brenda Phipps suggested hopefully.

'Yes, I do,' the reply came emphatically. 'Suicide or murder? There's still a doubt, but the pathologist has got to come down on one side or the other. I want us all there, we mustn't miss anything. We've got to know what happened for certain.'

The high multi-layered levels of glass and grey concrete that made up Addenbrooke's Hospital in Cambridge glowed brightly with all the vitality of the sick and the still living.

The part of the complex concerned with those who had exceeded their lifespan was low-built and unobtrusive, away in a far corner of the site, and shielded by a small leafless copse of silver birch trees.

The mortuary office was already crowded, even before the arrival of Packstone, Walsh and his team.

Detective Constable Alison Knott felt an intruder in this company of photographers, forensic scientists and others whom she did not even recognize, and she pressed herself firmly against the wall as though to make her rather chunky body completely unobtrusive.

In that she was unsuccessful. Walsh's sweeping glance round those present picked her out, and although clearly surprised to see her there, he motioned for her to join his group, much as a genial considerate host would draw a lone guest at a party into the social activity.

'I thought you were off duty, Alison,' Walsh said pleasantly.

'I am, but I asked Reg if I could come, and, well, I haven't done a full autopsy before,' she answered huskily, speaking for some reason in a voice a tone lower than normal.

'Good for you. You stick with Reg then, he'll tell you what's going on, but talk quietly, this pathologist gets a bit ratty if he has to shout to make himself heard.'

'Ready for identification,' came a flat expressionless voice from the doorway. The steel-haired phlegmatic mortuary attendant in grey nylon overalls promptly turned away and disappeared.

'You two stay here. Come on, Brenda,' Walsh said as he followed Packstone and several others out of the office.

'Mrs King and her mother have obviously arrived,' Reg explained. 'The body has to be formally identified to the satisfaction of the pathologist before he'll start the autopsy. That's done in the little chapel across the corridor. It can get a bit emotional in there. In a case like this, where the relative doing the identification might turn out to be on a murder suspect list, the boss likes to see their reactions. Brenda's already met her, so her opinion can be useful too.'

'Won't the pathologist take our word as to who the body is, then?' Alison asked.

'Oh no. The pathologist is a completely independent examiner. He works for the Home Office, not for us. There are fewer than thirty like him in the whole of England, believe it or believe it not. Anyway, this autopsy isn't being done for our benefit – the pathologist works at the behest of the coroner, and that's who his official report goes to. He has to witness the identification of the body and be satisfied in his own mind that it's genuine, or else there'd be no logical continuity when he has to produce his evidence in court. The pathologist is the short grey-haired man with the beaky nose,' Finch went on. 'The body then goes into the mortuary proper for the external examination. That's all right, but the internal one can get a bit hairy unless you've got a cast-iron stomach. If you feel gaggy, Alison, go outside and get some fresh air, it's nothing to be ashamed of. There're plenty who find they're not as tough as they think they are when a man's insides get spread all over the table.'

A little later the pathologist came back, now garbed in voluminous plastic protective clothing. 'Is everyone here authorized to attend?' he asked of the attendant. He received a nod in reply. 'Right, let's go in and get started.'

'Everyone settle down, let's have some quiet,' he continued. 'Now, the deceased has been identified as one Arthur C. King, aged thirty-two, and with no known ailments,' the pathologist said to his stenographer. 'His height is five feet eleven and he weighs approximately twelve and a half stone. The body was taken from the house where it had been found, with my authority and under my supervision. Before removal, however, I withdrew a weapon, a bronze sword, exhibit A1, from the body, and took hand and fingernail swabs for examination and analysis. Right, now, let's get to work.'

Alison found it difficult to concentrate for the next hour or so. The photographers seemed the most active of those there. As each item of Arthur King's clothing was removed, photos were taken, and while all this was going on the pathologist gave a detailed running commentary on what he was doing, in a monotonously inexpressive voice.

Dr Packstone stood watching close by the pathologist, but there was no reason yet to enliven the proceedings with questions, or any unexpected revelations. The only highlight of interest at this stage was when one of Packstone's staff came in to hand him a folded, written note. Packstone's face remained expressionless when he had read it, and so too did the pathologist's, but Walsh's contained a gleam of satisfaction as he handed the note to Reg Finch.

'Sword pommel,' Alison read, 'crevices of decorative glass mountings – traces of hair and skin. Need body samples – ASAP,' and it was signed simply, 'Jim'.

The removal of the remaining garments proceeded with a ritualistic solemnity, until the body was completely naked. Then the dead man's flesh was subjected to a meticulous examination, starting at his feet, and working up past the chest wound, to the head. Then the body was turned over on its face, and the process repeated.

Eventually, all the attention and the bright spotlights were concentrated on the back of Arthur King's head. The pathologist carefully eased the dark hair back, like a school nurse searching for unwanted visitors on the heads of young children.

'An impact contusion – recent and inflicted with some force. Surface area – a circle of about an inch and a half diameter,' the pathologist announced finally, straightening his back and taking up a tape measure so that he could plot the precise position relative to the ears, the bridge of the nose, and the nape of the neck.

'I'll shave these and have some photos done, then we can all have a break,' he said looking at Richard Packstone. 'That'll give you the samples you want. Quite straightforward, so far. There was nothing near where he lay that might have caused a contusion like that naturally, so it rather looks as though he was hit on the head with the pommel of that sword, to render him unconscious before the point was used to render the *coup de grâce*. Don't record that, that's just an observation,' he said to his stenographer. 'Right! Now some coffee.'

The expressions on her colleagues' faces, Alison decided, were smiles of relief, now that the vexed question of whether it was a murder or a suicide had apparently been resolved.

'It's not conclusive until we hear that the body traces on the sword pommel are from King, of course,' Walsh said cheerfully.

'And that's if the blood and urine samples don't contain drugs or show that King had drunk large quantities of alcohol, boss,' Reg Finch commented.

'But it does explain why the pommel and grip of the sword had been wiped clean of fingerprints, Chief,' Brenda ventured. 'That's been worrying me. If the killer had been wearing gloves it didn't make sense, but now it does.'

'You mean the sword was gripped by the blade and used as a club to knock him out before killing him,' Alison mused, 'so it was wiped to remove any traces from King's head. The killer was a bit naïve then, it would have been better to put a plastic bag over the end of the sword first.'

'You're not the killer, Alison,' Reg replied. 'If that was a mistake, let's hope there're more. One thing is for certain, King couldn't have hit himself on the head with that sword, not there.'

'True! He was probably sitting in that chair by the fire, and the killer crept up behind him. Someone else was definitely in that room, but how the devil did he get out?' Brenda pondered.

'Time enough for that later. Packstone will sort that out,' Walsh said emphatically. The results of all the various tests were only a few hours away, and there was probably a whole wealth of useful information to come from the meticulous forensic examination of the house in Badon Lane, so it was pointless to speculate on the means and the method at this moment.

'Regardless of how the murder was contrived,' he went on, 'there must be a substantial motive behind it. We've got two immediate suspects – Mrs King, who might have got rid of an unwanted husband, and there's the death threat. There's still time tonight for work to be done on those. Brenda, you go and talk to Professor Hughes at Downing College about undergraduate involvement in animal rights activities and Reg, you find out Mrs King's movements last night, so that we can start checking on her. Then tomorrow morning first thing, we'll meet in my office. There'll be the photos and videos to go through, and a whole lot more. I'll stay on here, I've nothing better to do. I think we've learned pretty well all we're going to from this autopsy, but you can never be certain. Are you going to stay and keep me company, Alison?'

With Gwen away from home, he did have nothing better to do. He'd need to iron a clean shirt for the morning, of course, but he wasn't going to hurry away to an empty home for that.

There were fewer people in the examination room now, so Alison was able to get closer and see better.

68

The pathologist selected a knife, and deftly made a deep incision from ear to ear over the head, then from beneath the chin of the body, right down the chest and stomach to the pubis. White flesh instantly changed to bloody meat.

It was then that Alison Knott decided that she was tired – that the day had already been a long one and that it might be wise to get a good night's sleep in preparation for another busy day tomorrow. So she expained to Detective Chief Inspector Sidney Walsh before she left.

Walsh nodded his agreement, but he inwardly smiled before concentrating back on the matter in hand. It was quite likely that sleep would not come too easily for Alison Knott that night.

For a Serious Crime team, a murder inquiry meant that the realities of death were part of the realities of life. Some people, like the pathologist, hospital casualty staff and soldiers in war, might become callously indifferent to it all, but even they had to start somewhere.

7

'Come into the warm, my dear. Let me take your coat.' The cheerful rotund figure of Professor Edwin Hughes ushered Brenda Phipps into his luxurious Downing College rooms. 'Are you well? You look as fit as a fiddle; but that's hardly an apt description of anyone, is it? Unless, of course, they're sensitive and highly strung.'

'I'm very well, thank you, Professor. I am sorry to disturb your evening. You must get thoroughly sick of us bothering you; but you're so very useful, you know so much of what goes on in the university,' she said, bestowing a radiantly disarming smile on the friendly academic who had played such a useful role in solving some of the Cambridgeshire Constabulary's problems in the past.

Hughes smiled back. 'It's nice to know that an old fogey

like me still has his uses, but I don't mind you coming to me with your problems at all. No, not in the least. They help broaden my horizons and keep me in touch with the real world, or some part of it. One can get very narrow-minded and detached, being constantly in a college environment, you know. Cabined, cribbed, confined, you might say. No, I'm only too pleased to help, and how can I help you now?'

Brenda explained about Arthur King's death threat and from where it had supposedly originated.

'Oh dear. Well, I do hope this turns out to be a false line of inquiry,' the elderly professor said, pulling thoughtfully on his plump chins. 'Such publicity would not be welcome. In general the animal rights movements do much good work as pressure groups, to curb the worst excesses of cruelty. Extremes of enthusiasm do occur with young undergraduates at times, but I hope this is not one of them. There are many action groups and societies within the university, of course, and tomorrow I will seek out the names of some sensible members of them for you to interview. However, having said that – and I do not wish to appear presumptuous by diverting you from your line of approach to your investigations, of course – it does seem to me that your problem could well involve a much wider field than just students in Cambridge. In that respect, I do have a friend who might be able to help you. He lives not far away – in Ely, as a matter of fact. You'll find him a charming man, and quite ready to help if he's approached in a sensible way. He's a physicist turned computer expert, who commutes regularly to London, but he is also a committee member of one of the national animal rights movements. Would you like me to ring him and see if he's at home? I thought you might. You young things are so energetic. You should adopt Admiral Nelson's motto of "Waste not an hour", I think. It would be most appropriate.'

Reg Finch parked his car outside the semi-detached pebble-dashed house. Before getting out he opened his black case and, in the light of a nearby street lamp, made a note of the time, twenty-fifteen hours, on the top of the pad. He also made sure that he had several statement forms available. Then he closed the case, got out of the car and walked slowly down the front path.

It was a very sobering experience, having been in the presence of a dead man for several hours, particularly one whose life had been ended so abruptly. It made one reflect on one's own life, on what one had achieved, and who would genuinely mourn one's passing. Reginald Finch had had a choice of several careers. He'd been well educated and was from a well-to-do family, with all the connections that would have given him a good start as a City lawyer, or banker, or in some business. But to his family's surprise and disappointment, he'd opted to join the police force, in which they had no influence to open doors and ease the passage of promotion. Perhaps that had been the challenge, to stand on his own feet and fight to make his own place in the world. It had not been easy going, and many times he had come within an ace of chucking it in. Then he had the opportunity to work with Detective Inspector Walsh, as he was then, in the CID. A move never yet regretted, for this was a niche that suited him well. The subtle, methodical pitting of his wits against the criminal mind, in order to bring before the law those who broke it to further their own ends, suited him well. Arthur King's naked body, lying ignominiously on the mortuary table, reflected the extreme of criminal cases – murder. The act that no punishment, counselling, compensation or fine could reverse.

The motives in this particular case must be very strong, because considerable ingenuity must have been exercised in the planning to make it look as much like suicide as it did. No unpremeditated fiery emotional flare-up this.

A child's scooter lay on the path, and in the uncertain light Reg Finch nearly tripped over it.

Before he'd even rung the bell, the front door was opened by an anxious-looking middle-aged woman.

'Thank God, you've come,' she said. 'She's in here.'

Finch found himself being hustled into the small front room

just off the tiny hallway. He looked round it in surprise. Most of the space was taken up by a wardrobe, a chest of drawers and a single bed – and in that bed, propped up on several pillows, was a very elderly woman.

The skin of her face was a sallow grey, stretched parchment-tight over the bones beneath. She made a low gurgling noise in her throat as she breathed, and her eyes, although they appeared to be looking at her visitor, were lustreless and dull. The rattling sounds from her half-open mouth became croaking sounds as she tried to speak.

His presence seemed expected and needed, and Reg Finch bent forward solicitously to try and hear what she was saying and unaccountably found himself sitting on the bedside chair. A withered wrinkled talon of a hand reached out to close over his.

'Is there really a heaven up there?' the voice seemed to ask, and the rheumy eyes looking up at his face now seemed anxious and fearful.

Finch swallowed nervously, desperately seeking the right words of comfort for the situation in which he had suddenly found himself.

He'd seen death before, in many forms, and of necessity was hardened to it to some degree. But he had just come from the presence of one who was certainly dead, and into the presence of one for whom the sands of time were clearly running out, and his emotional defences were completely unprepared.

A wave of instinctive compassion took over his mind and swamped methodical reasoning.

'Heaven is a wonderful place, so I'm told,' he said softly, while blinking back the tears that were trying to form in the corners of his own eyes. 'It's a place of peace and happiness. Where there's no pain or sickness, or arguments and rows, and all the people waiting to greet you are those you've known and loved, who have gone there before you.' He put his other hand over hers and pressed reassuringly. For a moment he wasn't sure if she had understood what he'd said, but then her eyes seemed to flash with a momentary smile of contentment, as though she had heard what she wished to hear.

The creases round her mouth relaxed and her eyelids slowly closed, as if there was now no need to keep them open. The rasping breathing became softer and more regular but the intervals between the laboured gasps were noticeably longer. 'We're all here with you. You're not alone,' Finch whispered several times, unable to stir and not wanting a stony silence to break the thread of communication, if indeed there was any.

Ten minutes later there came no more feeble gasps, and the fingers between his hands ceased to flutter.

Finch laid that still hand on the bed cover, and stood up. 'I'm sorry,' he said lamely to the grieving woman who sobbed quietly into her handkerchief by the doorway.

'I've been expecting it, doctor, ever since she had that last heart attack, but even so . . . now . . . it's still a shock. I'll be all right in a minute. You'll have to tell me what to do now. I don't know. My dad died when I was young, you see.'

'I'm not –' Reg Finch started to say, but the ringing of the door bell and the arrival of the real doctor postponed the need for explanations.

'You were ever so good with her, Sergeant. I'm so grateful. I know she died happy. I could see that,' Mrs Killibury said as Finch went out of the front door.

'I'll come back tomorrow to see your daughter, if that's all right,' he said, as he started to walk back down the path, carefully avoiding the scooter.

To pursue a murder investigation under the conditions that that household was experiencing at the moment was definitely not on. The wisest thing to do was to go home and get a good night's sleep, ready for what should be a very active and interesting day tomorrow.

But sleep did not come easily, even though he had the warm companionship of his wife, Margaret, in his bed. When sleep did come, it was restless and confused, with fleeting dreams of bony hands, and autopsies being done in a sweet-smelling heavenly morgue by people whose white flowing robes unaccountably showed no traces of blood.

In another house in the city, Detective Chief Inspector Walsh also dozed fitfully, until disturbed by a welcome long-distance telephone call from his wife Gwen, after which he slept more soundly.

Earlier that evening, Ely was shrouded in a misty haze, as it often was in winter. The surrounding low-lying fields regularly flood, and produce those swirling clouds of fine white vapour that drift across the city and all the fens, when the saturated air condenses in the cool of the night.

In the centre of the city, beyond the wide grassed fore-court, floodlights illuminated an ethereal cathedral façade, whose soaring carved stones seemed not to stand solidly on the ground, but to float on low smoky clouds. Yet it all dwarfed and made so puny the giant black cannon that stood incongruously guarding the entrance path against earth-bound mortals.

Not far away, Dr Julian Lancelot Fry lived in a mellow red-brick Georgian house, set back from the mews-like cul-de-sac, behind high, intricately wrought, iron railings.

He answered the door to Brenda Phipps' ring, and greeted her politely but rather curtly. He was a neat, dapper, still handsome man with a shock of over-long grey-white hair, and aged, she thought, well into his sixties. He wore black Chelsea boots, designer blue jeans with a heavily buckled leather belt and a black quilted body-warmer over a black roll-necked sweater. Unlike his friend Professor Hughes, he looked physically fit – but he had a streaming cold.

'You'd better sit over there, well away from me,' he sniffed, pointing to a floral-patterned, loose-covered comfortable arm-chair on the far side of the gas fire. 'I really don't know why I said I'd see you at all,' he muttered huskily. 'I wouldn't have if it hadn't been for Edwin. I hope you don't want to stay too long. I feel like death warmed up.'

'I'll try not to. Have you taken something for your cold?' Brenda asked sympathetically, sneaking a good look round the over-warm spacious room. It contained several glass-fronted cabinets. Most of the shelves contained books, but others held a collection of millefiori paperweights and porcelain figurines.

'I've had the usual. Beecham's, aspirin with hot rum and lemon, but it doesn't matter what you take; colds always run their course. A day to come, a day there and a day to go, usually. You've just got to grin and bear it. You interested in paperweights?' he asked. He could hardly fail to notice her interest.

'Yes indeed,' Brenda replied enthusiastically. 'They're lovely, but so is that little piece of Dresden.' She pointed to a white china shepherdess.

'Dresden, you reckon. What about the soldier on the shelf above?' He sniffed.

'Later Meissen, seen from here. It looks right, but there're many fakes.'

'That one isn't. So, you know a good piece when you see one,' he said approvingly, studying her face with more interest. 'Phipps, Detective Constable, a pretty young thing who knows her porcelain,' he mused thoughtfully. 'Old Hughes has mentioned you several times, and your two colleagues whose names I can't remember. You got him involved in some of your murder cases, didn't you? He enjoyed that, often talks about them.'

Brenda nodded and smiled. Clearly, having the professor as a mutual acquaintance was a good point in her favour, but a few subtle questions to show an interest in his main line of business might well improve on the general good impression she appeared to have made.

'I gather you're something of a guru in computer circles, Dr Fry. That sounds very interesting,' she prompted.

'Guru? I don't know about that. I ought to know a bit about them, I've rather grown up with them,' Fry acknowledged. 'In the early days systems and programming were considered "the thing", but now we've got computer programs a child could handle, and programs that write programs. So nowadays I just solve problems, the bigger the better, mainly man-made ones. They've got me on this pension scheme fraud business at the moment, trying to dig out of what data is left, the details of transactions that someone else has deliberately tried to wipe off the record. Most programs have got some sort of retrieval ability built in, simply to guard against accidental loss by human operative error, you see, but you need to know what you're doing. It's a bit like being given a chess-board layout at the checkmate stage, and from that, working out what all the previous moves were. Fraud cases are my main concern, there're plenty of those to keep me busy.' He pulled a clean handkerchief from his trouser pocket and blew on a reddened nose that looked distinctly sore. 'That, and sorting out the aftermath of computer viruses, of course.'

'Computer viruses? You mean when someone writes a deliberate fault into a program that's timed to go off some time later, and which throws the whole system into chaos?'

'Yes, that's putting it very simply, of course,' Dr Fry said, now showing some enthusiasm for the conversation. 'The motivation of the individual doing such a thing can be quite complicated. A disgruntled employee might take his revenge by amending a program so that six months after he's left, all the stored data is wiped off completely. Companies rely on their computers so intensely nowadays that any disruption to their systems can be a disaster, but there are other ways of messing things up. Imagine the effect if a computer suddenly starts printing out a two instead of a nine, or a one for a six. How quickly would that be detected? All the cheques that went out, the wages and the invoices, would all be wrong.' He took a sip of his rum and lemon. 'I've been developing a program that can act like the antibodies in the bloodstream and can search out and destroy viruses,' he announced proudly.

Brenda saw the opportunity for an intelligent comment. 'Ah!' she said wisely. 'You'll be able to sell that to all the big computer operators. You'll make a fortune.'

'Indeed, I might.'

'Fascinating!' Brenda exclaimed, but it was now time to turn the conversation to the real reason for her being there. 'Dr Fry, I think you could help us. Last night a man was found murdered in his home. He was a research scientist, testing new drugs and medicines. Some time ago he received a letter condemning him to death, because he was supposed to use animals in his work. Obviously we must try to find out who wrote it. I understand from Professor Hughes that you might be able to give us the names of some of the extremists who might do such a thing.'

The question brought on a bout of sneezing, but eventually Fry asked, 'And who was this dead man?'

'Dr Arthur King.'

Fry nodded slowly. 'He worked with Parkinson and that lot near the Science Park. I wouldn't have thought they were on anyone's action list. The recognized societies would never do such a thing, of course, but there are anarchists and extremists who try to work their way in and cause trouble for their own political ends. They're weeded out as soon as they're spotted. Let me think.'

After a few moments' cogitation he got to his feet and took a few folders and a notebook from one of the bookcases, then he sat down again, to flip though the pages and occasionally to write things down.

'There you are, young lady,' he said eventually, handing her a sheet of paper. 'I'm no criminal psychologist, and I might be doing some on that list a grave injustice, but they are people we've rejected because of their activities in other areas.' He sneezed and fumbled for his handkerchief again. 'I don't wish to be rude, but I think you'll have to go now. I'll be better in my nice warm bed, I think. I hope you don't catch my cold.'

There was time, Brenda thought, to call in to her office in Headquarters and write up the reports of her visits before going home. The Chief wanted an early start tomorrow and there was obviously going to be plenty to do.

In her office was a cheap word processor, quicker by far than the typewriter – or, even worse, longhand.

However, she found that her office was being used. Detective Constable Arthur Bryant had most of the statements taken in the Badon Lane house-to-house inquiry spread all over her desk, but one of them he was studying intently.

'For Pete's sake, Arthur, do you always have to make such a mess whenever you're doing something?' Brenda demanded. 'How long are you going to be? I've got a report to write.'

'That's a nice welcome, that is,' Arthur retorted. 'I'm doing the summary report of all these statements we've taken in Fulbourn today, but I've got a funny one here. I'm not quite sure what to do with it.'

'What's the matter with it?' Brenda inquired.

'It's an old lady, a widow, I think. Anyway she lives on her own, two doors down from King's place. Got a house full of canaries. Must have twenty at least, all over the place. You could hear them chirping a mile –'

'Get to the point, Arthur,' Brenda said irritably. 'I'm in no mood for your ramblings.'

'I'm not rambling,' he protested.

'Well, what's funny about this woman? Lots of people keep pet birds.'

'Birds have got nothing to do with it, Brenda. What are you going on about birds for?' Arthur shook his head in confusion. 'All I said was that she kept canaries. No, this woman doesn't sleep well. She gets up and wanders round the house quite often during the night. She says she saw, but she doesn't know what the time was, because she don't wear a watch, you see –'

'What did she see, Arthur?'

'She says it was a big black dog, Brenda, with fiery eyes and a drooling mouth. Those are her words. When I saw her statement I went and talked with her myself. Fiery eyes and drooling mouth, and it walked right across her lawn, she says. It stopped in the middle and seemed to look straight at her, then it pottered off. Quite scared her. She said it was the harbinger of doom, that dog. You see, what's so crazy is that she insists it left no prints in the snow as it went. That's what's so funny about it.'

'It was pitch dark, in the middle of the night, Arthur. So how could she see anything outside, let alone a dog that left no prints in the snow? Did you ask her that?' Brenda demanded.

'Of course I did. The lights downstairs were left on, so the lawn was lit up, she says.'

'Is it likely, Arthur? Those birds would be chirping all night if that was the case. She'd never get any sleep.'

'Oh no. Each cage has got its own cover. I saw them myself. Each one's embroidered with the bird's name too. No, I believe she saw a dog, but should I point out this statement in my report to the Inspector as being of particular note; or will he think it's silly?'

'No footprints in the snow? The dog the Chief and I followed definitely left tracks. So she thinks she saw Old Shuck, does she?' Brenda mused thoughtfully.

'Old Shuck? Who's he?'

'Old Shuck's a ghost dog that wanders about Norfolk, and presumably around here as well, bringing death, gloom and destruction in his wake. He's quite frequently seen by drunks, and lonely old ladies who keep canaries. They seem to survive the experience all right. The Chief'll want to know, Arthur. There's a big dog in this case somewhere, but as I say, that one did leave tracks. Get your report finished, then I can do mine.'

'The old lady said it left no tracks – I didn't,' Arthur Bryant announced as he turned back to the word processor and started tapping at the keyboard. 'I looked at the middle of her lawn in daylight, you see. Some dog had stopped there all right. It had left a blooming great pile of –'

'Make a note of that as well, Arthur.'

8

'The traces of hair and skin trapped in the settings of the stones on the sword pommel are definitely from that contusion on the back of King's head,' Walsh announced next morning when the three of them had congregated in the viewing-room annexe in the photography department at Headquarters. 'And the pathologist's report will also state categorically that the man's arms were not long enough for his hands to have gripped the hilt in the way the prints indicated, not before the sword had been driven into his chest. So they must have been applied later – when he was already dead. Packstone was quite right. We do have a full-scale murder inquiry on our hands.'

'What about drugs or poisons in his blood or on that piece of cheese he'd bitten?' Reg asked.

'None. No traces of anything like that. One other thing, Grigson was correct about it being a Volvo that rammed him. The analysis of the paint left on Grigson's car ties up with the manufacturer's specification, but it's probably an oldish model, since it had been resprayed once already. Now, let's start on these videos. The ones from the house's surveillance system first. You work the machine, Brenda.'

The pictures that came up on the screen showed the date and the time of initiation, in a narrow band across the top, but that particular camera seemed to have been little used. During the five days until the night of King's death, up to the moment when the Cambridgeshire Constabulary's Scene of Crime team approached the side door, preparing to force an entry, the only recorded movements, to or from, were those of three cats, and the owner, Arthur King himself.

'Right, there's something wrong with that camera, obviously,' Walsh said. 'The cats were recorded and so was King, but we know for certain that a dog went along there too. Why doesn't that show?'

'Maybe the dog was Old Shuck, Chief. Maybe he can be seen and leave no tracks one minute, then leave tracks and not be seen another.'

'Thank you, Brenda. Let's keep our feet firmly on the ground this morning,' Walsh instructed.

'Old Shuck did, in King's drive, apparently,' Brenda replied with a smile.

'Next video, please. The front door camera.'

On this there was more activity, with postmen, newspaper deliverers and . . .

'Stop it there, go back a few seconds,' Walsh demanded as

two people, probably the occupants of the Volvo, appeared, striding across the line of vision. The camera, mounted high on the wall and angled down, was obviously set to record anyone or anything approaching the front door, and that it clearly did, since the walls of the house could be seen to either side, but its forward range of vision was restricted, and it could not see out as far as the drive or the main gate.

Brenda slowed the video speed right down this time. The intruders were obviously men and, even in that stunted foreshortened view, both were taller than average. They appeared to be wearing trainers, jeans and parkas; their facial features were muffled by scarves or masks. It was much the same a few frames later as they reappeared, retracing their steps somewhat faster than they had come.

'Can you run that all again but showing a close-up of just their faces?' Walsh asked.

Brenda confidently moved things and tapped keys on the keyboard. On the rerun it appeared that one of the two men may have had a dark moustache, but there was little else either facially or on their clothing which might be an aid to identification. Then they watched the salesman, Mervyn Grigson, and the patrol car sergeant come and play their parts in the saga.

The other outside videos were made as the Scene of Crime photographers had circled round the house while the snow had still lain upon the ground. Other than a few marks made by the tiny feet of birds or rats there were no other tracks in the snow at the back and far side of the house.

'So, until those two characters went to the front window, there were no tracks to be seen on that side of the house,' Reg observed thoughtfully.

'And the other security camera shows King himself making the only footprints going to the side door,' Brenda went on, 'and that was while it was still snowing, because they were barely visible later on when the SOC videoed the dog prints.'

'Logically, then, the photographic evidence tells us that King's killer must have entered the house before it started snowing, and presumably he left under our very noses, because it must have been after we'd got there.' Walsh made that proposal while shaking his head doubtfully.

'That may be a logical deduction, Chief, but it falls down because the alarm system was active inside the house as well as outside. No one could have moved about in there,' Brenda explained.

'And there was no one in there when the SOC arrived, except King himself. They searched the place, and they're not daft,' Reg stated positively.

'What if the killer is one of the SOC team, Chief? He might have been in there already and joined his mates during the search. They'd think he came in with them, wouldn't they?'

'It's doubtful, but we'll have to check – and we'd still have to explain why the security system didn't pick him up. Don't forget, Packstone says it was working perfectly,' Walsh said.

'The side door camera wasn't working perfectly, or else we'd have seen the dog,' Brenda replied.

'Those dog tracks just circled round in the wood and came back, did they, boss?' Reg asked.

'They appeared to, yes. There was a lot of confusion just outside the gate where the snow had been churned up and I didn't pick up any tracks leading to Bryant's canary lover, but because of the conditions, I can't put my hand on my heart and say for certain there weren't any,' Walsh replied.

Reg nodded. 'There's a farm track on the other side of that wood, but the dog tracks didn't go that far then?'

'No! They went as far as a big oak, and then came back,' Walsh said emphatically. 'It seems to me that our own thinking is going round in circles, but that's because we're trying to make sense only of those facts that we know, and obviously we don't know enough yet. We can safely leave the technology of the security system to Packstone. He's got enough experts to call on. Our job is to concentrate on Arthur King. We need to build up a picture of the kind of man he was, and we do that by talking to relatives and friends, and we seek out areas of conflict in his past, or anything that might be considered a motive for murder. Then we'll construct a suspect list and see how the alibis fit with the evidence.

King's wife should be a mine of information – how did you get on with her, Reg?

Finch explained why he'd gathered no information from that source.

'I understand,' Walsh nodded. 'Right, let's have a plan of action. I'll go and see Mrs King. Brenda, you interview the sister who lives in Norfolk. Reg, you follow up on the writer of some of those old letters, the man living in Newmarket. He must have been a close friend. I'm particularly interested in finding out about King's lady friends, that sort of thing always makes for a good motive. In the mean time I'll see the builder who did the alterations to King's house, and the chappie who installed the burglar alarm. Brenda, you've got the animal rights leads to work on. What with the names you learned last night and those on the list that Parkinson from King's laboratory has sent in, you'll be busy. You've got that woman doctor's call-outs to check as well. You can set young Bryant on those. Reg, you've got the Volvo to find. I want to talk to those two characters. Any questions?'

'Yes,' Reg said thoughtfully. 'There's another pattern in all this that might be worth following up. We've got a King, whose name is Arthur, being killed with his own sword which is called Excalibur; and he was married to a Gwenda, which is pretty near to being Guinevere. Add to that the fact that her maiden name was Killibury, which is not far from Tintagel Castle which some people believe was King Arthur's Camelot.' Finch drummed his long bony fingers on the top of his document case. 'There's more. King's house is called Glein House, and is down Badon Lane. Glein and Badon were the sites of two of Arthur's battles – at least I think they were. I've never been all that interested in these Arthur stories, because there's little real history in them, but nevertheless, you can see what I mean. There's a theme that seems to run strongly through this case.'

'The chap I saw last night is a Lancelot, Reg,' Brenda ventured, her eyes alive with humour. With Reg's interest in archaeology, it was typical of him to latch on to a historic theme like that.

Walsh sought his pipe, and pondered while he filled it. 'The way you've put it makes sense,' he said eventually. 'The weird circumstances of this case are going to take some pretty weird explanations. Follow it up by all means.'

'I've two names of extremists on the list Dr Fry gave me, Reg. Mark Ambrose and Gerald Sinclair. Ambrosius and Geraint – they're both Arthurian names, aren't they?' Brenda proposed, with a very broad grin.

She was feeling cheerful. Between them they'd quite a number of people to interview. What was so exciting was the possibility that when they'd finished seeing all those on the list, one of them might actually have spoken to Arthur King's murderer. Perhaps it would be her.

The occupants of the Killiburys' pebble-dashed semi-detached home on the estate near the hospital were all distinctly gloomy and depressed.

The rear room in which the family lived was hardly suit-able for Walsh's purpose, so he interviewed Mrs King in the small single bedroom upstairs. He sat on a hard yellow-painted wooden chair, while she sat, more comfortably, on the bed.

Mrs Gwenda King was a slim young woman in her late twenties, with short fair hair of loose curls, a slightly snubby nose and strikingly pretty facial features. She was not very tall, barely above the 'five foot two, eyes of blue' of the old song, but any signs of an energetic vivacity were lacking this morning. Her large blue eyes focused clearly and her soft musical voice was well modulated, suggesting that she'd had a good education.

'It's difficult to come to terms with it all, Inspector,' she said. 'One minute someone is there, a solid part of reality, then out of the blue comes the news that I no longer have a husband, and my children no longer have a father, and now my grandma's gone as well.'

Walsh studied her face with the intensity of a psychologist in session with a patient. 'You still had deep feelings for your husband, even though you'd only recently left him?' he prompted, trying to direct her thoughts.

Gwenda King looked down at her delicate little hands lying loosely clasped in her lap. 'Yes, I suppose so. Arthur was one of those men a woman can both love and hate at the same time. I've given a lot of thought recently to how I felt about him, so if I appear to be casual, that's far from the truth. When I met him I thought he was the most wonderful man in the world. Charming, as well as being very physically attractive. I'd only known him a few months before he asked me to marry him. I was a bit surprised at the time, because, being a mere school-teacher, I didn't think I fitted into his life-style, but I didn't hesitate in saying yes. Perhaps I should have done, because there was another side to his character I didn't know then.'

'What was that?'

'Well, it's difficult to put into words, but he was so self-centred that he could be cruelly hard on people, even his friends. His sister, for instance. She fell in love with an Ethiopian and married him. Arthur disapproved of mixed marriages, and so he just cut her out of his life, and wouldn't have any more to do with her. He just drew a curtain and blocked out anything he didn't like. It was the same with his friend, Robin, and it was Robin who introduced us. They'd known each other since their college days, but when Robin said something in fun about the King Arthur stories, he got the same treatment. Cut off and totally ignored. If Arthur didn't like something, then for him it didn't exist any more.'

'Robin lives in Newmarket, doesn't he? Did you meet many of his old friends?' Walsh asked.

Gwenda King shook her head. 'No, not really. Arthur appeared to change his style of life when we married, you see, except for his other women, but I didn't know that then.'

Walsh nodded solemly. 'How did you find out?'

'I had a letter, an anonymous letter, a couple of months or so ago. It said that Arthur had been having affairs with other women ever since the day he'd married me. It wasn't worded viciously or nastily. It just said that I ought to know the truth; and if I didn't believe it, then I should watch outside the flat of Anita Grant, she's one of the people Arthur worked with, on the following evening. So I did just that. I told him I'd be spending the night here with mum and I borrowed my dad's old car so that I wouldn't be spotted. I parked a little way down the road from Anita Grant's flat. Sure enough, out he came at about elevenish, all smug and well satisfied. He told me the next day he'd been to one of his Arthurian Society meetings.' Gwenda's face looked dolefully resigned. 'The scales seemed to fall away from my eyes, then,' she went on. 'I found I couldn't view the future objectively, not living with and being touched by a man I couldn't trust. There would be no happiness for me, only misery, so I knew I had to make the break and the sooner the better, for all concerned.'

'Was this before or after you moved to Badon Lane?' Walsh wanted to know.

'Just before,' the other replied, 'and that was another thing. After he'd received that death threat Arthur became quite neurotic about security. The security system Arthur was having installed in Badon Lane was far more restrictive than the one we had in the old house; so that became another reason for leaving him. I was a bit of a coward when I did that. I couldn't tell him I was leaving, not face to face, so when he'd gone off to work one morning, I just packed up everything we needed and left him a note. Do you know, he never once came round here to talk to me, or to see the children. I didn't want him to, of course, but I thought at least he'd try. He just drew a curtain on us too, blocking us out of his life. I knew I'd hurt his ego by leaving, but I never dreamt he could be so callous as to reject his own children.' Tears appeared in her eyes and she had to bite her bottom lip with her small white teeth.

'So you never actually lived in the new house in Badon Lane then?' Walsh asked, rather hastily.

'No. It wasn't a new house, of course. Early Victorian, I think, and it needed quite a lot of work doing to it. There was rot in some of the floors and roof timbers, the surveyor said; but there was lots of potential and it's a lovely situation. The builders just about gutted the place. I didn't have a lot to do with that, but I did organize the decorations – the colour schemes for each room, and I chose the curtains and carpets. It would have looked very nice when it was done, I think.' Mrs King seemed back in control of herself again.

'You planned where the sword, shield and ancient helmet were to be displayed, did you?' Walsh asked cautiously.

'Those horrible things? Oh no! We had them stuck in the hall at the other place, with that spooky wooden chest. I wouldn't have given them house-room, myself, but Arthur thought they were marvellous. He picked them up years ago, long before I'd met him, in one of those shops down the Brighton Lanes. He probably hung them over the mantelpiece in the sitting-room, knowing him.'

'We know about your husband's death threat. Had he made any other enemies?' Walsh asked.

Gwenda King shook her head. 'Not to my knowledge.'

'Did you keep the anonymous letter, the one telling you about your husband's other women?'

'I'm not sure. Perhaps it's somewhere in one of my suitcases. Why, do you want it?'

'It could be useful.'

'I'll look for it this afternoon. I'll give you a ring if I find it.'

'Thank you.' Walsh smiled. 'Now, I apologize for doing so, but to do my job properly I do have to ask you where you were, who you were with, and what you were doing the night your husband died.'

Mrs King nodded understandingly, and gave a slight rueful smile. 'I was here, of course, but when the children were in bed I did go down to Sainsbury's to do some shopping. About seven o'clock, that would have been. I might have been out about an hour, not that long, probably.'

'Did your mother go with you?'

She gave him a reproachful look. 'Of course not. Dad was out playing darts. We can't leave the children on their own, not at their age.'

Downing College, in Cambridge, is mostly hidden away behind the row of tall shops that line one side of Regent Street and

St Andrew's Street, but a view of its inner quadrangle and stone buildings can be seen from the road, through a wide, elaborately worked wrought-iron gateway.

As it was only a short distance from Police Headquarters, across the wide expanse of grassed land known as Parker's Piece, Reg Finch had decided to walk.

'Do come in, Sergeant,' Professor Edwin Hughes said in his deep-toned voice, as he welcomed his second police visitor in two days. 'It's very nice of you to come and see me,' the professor went on, 'but as I said when you phoned, I've a tutorial in a little over an hour, so we might have to break off then.'

Reg Finch nodded. 'I quite understand, and I very much appreciate your making time to see me, but I've a rather unusual line of investigation to follow, and I –'

'Come over by the fire and sit down first,' the professor interrupted, waving a hand towards the far end of the room. 'We might as well be comfortable. Now, just how can I help you with your inquiries?'

'Well, we have a case of a man named Arthur King who was found stabbed in the heart by what appears to be a replica of a Romano-British sword, which had Excalibur etched on the blade,' Finch explained.

'Oh, really? That's certainly unusual, I should think,' the professor interrupted, his eyes bright with interest, and a curiously enigmatic smile hovering about his lips. 'Was this the same man who had received a death threat from a so-called animal rights organization?'

Finch looked surprised, and nodded his head. 'Of course, Brenda came to see you yesterday. I do hope we're not making nuisances of ourselves.'

'Not at all, I'm only too pleased to help in whatever way I can. Do go on,' the professor said politely.

'I thought a chat with you might help me to decide how best to ... well, let me explain. As I say, the man's name is Arthur C. King. The C stands for Caractacus, I think, but it's not the Celtic king who fought against the Claudian invasion by the Romans that might be important, but the King Arthur who fought the Danes nearly five hundred years later. His colleagues where he worked say that he was a bit of an Arthurian fanatic, you see, and he also had a wife named Gwenda. He lived in Glein House, in Badon Lane, and was writing a treatise to prove that Camelot was Cambridge Castle, because of the "Cam" bit, or it might have been out at Wandlebury; I'm not sure which yet. I haven't finished reading his manuscript and his arguments aren't clear anyway.'

The professor pulled a long face and held up his hands in mock horror. 'Oh lord! Not another one of those. The Celtic name for the Cam was Rae. That just means water, but whether the present name was in common usage by the Arthurian period, I've no idea. You know, we've just had a Danish author using place-names to prove that Wandlebury was really ancient Troy and the Greek ships weren't Greek, but French. They landed on a beach at Ely, because, he says, in those days the sea covered the fens; which I'm pretty sure it didn't, because sea levels then were fifty or sixty feet lower than they are now. The fens were once an oak forest, I believe. Farmers still plough up the trunks occasionally, don't they? Hardly a countryside suitable for chariot battles. Still, I interrupt, and I digress. I'm sorry.'

'Well, because of the Arthurian name associations, which you must admit are unusual, we thought, at least I did, that the motives in the case might have something to do with the stories; but before I wade through all the literature, I thought it would be wise to ask your opinion on what might be relevant,' Finch explained.

'Very wise, considering the vast amount that has been written – not that I'm an expert on the subject, you understand,' Hughes mused, rubbing his chin thoughtfully. 'Factually, there is little to go on, as you probably know. The first reference to an Arthur is in the *Historia Brittonum*, the earliest existing version of which is dated to the late eight hundreds. That says, if my memory is correct, that "Arthur fought against them," the Saxons, that is, "in those days, with the kings of the Britons, but he himself was leader of the battles." It then lists a series of battles, Glein, Badon,

Camlann and so on, which are also refered to by other early writers. The monk Gildas, who wrote in the sixth century, says that the leader of the British was Ambrosius Aurelianus, and that under him the battles went their way until the seige of Badon Hill, and he dates that precisely, as being in the year of his birth, somewhere between the years 490 and 510. Gildas doesn't mention Arthur, and neither do any other sources of the time. There are Continental references to a British king called Riotimus, but that's no help since the word merely means "High King". Geoffrey Ashe has written several books relating Arthur to this Riotimus, and he does very well too, but I'm afraid it's all really point-stretching. As I say, the earliest references to Arthur are as the leader in the battles, not as king, and Gildas ignores him completely. Myself, I suspect that some of the early writers, having to translate from the Welsh and Breton languages into French or Latin, may have taken the Welsh word *uthr*, or *Uther*, which means "terrible" or "the terrible one", simply as a name, because of its phonetic similarity to Arthur. It's not difficult to imagine such a confusion, is it? Well, there you are,' Hughes went on. 'That's a thumbnail sketch of the basic facts, and if you hold any firm opinions based on those, then it's more a matter of blind faith than real judgement.' Hughes waved his hands depreciatively. 'However, subsequent writers, Geoffrey of Monmouth especially, have had a field day with their imaginations. Merlin, Guinevere, the Knights of the Round Table, and so on. Ninty-nine per cent of all the words in the books about King Arthur are about the subsequent literature, because there's not enough real truth to fill a whole page. They'll tell you Arthur died of his battle wounds when his nephew Modred turned traitor and seduced Queen Guinevere. You could do worse than start by reading Ashe, when you've read Tennyson's and Malory's accounts of Arthur's death, but a chat with someone in the Arthurian Society might also help.'

The professor's face beamed an encouraging smile – but Finch's expression was decidedly more serious.

No Modred had turned up in the case, so far. If he wanted to follow up that aspect of the murder of Arthur King, there was obviously a great deal of reading and thinking to be done.

The narrow road had wide grass verges between the brambly hedgerows, and ran straight, up and over the gently undulating low north Norfolk hills.

Brenda Phipps slowed on the next rise. Far in the distance, away over vast fields tinted green with winter wheat, and under a sky of scudding dark clouds, there showed a streak of the grey North Sea.

In the next wooded valley she found the sign she was watching for. It read 'Medraut House – Pottery and Art Gallery – Visitors welcome.'

The driveway led to a shingled area by some red-brick out-houses and a low white stuccoed Queen Anne house with stunning country views.

'Come in. I'm Anna Selassie, Arthur King's sister. It was you who rang me earlier, was it?' The graceful, tall and beautiful woman was in her early forties, but what was really striking about her was her relaxed expression of serene contentment. She wore a clay-splashed flowered cotton overall over her jeans and sweater, but that was taken off before Brenda was shown into an elegant sitting-room that looked out over an extensive lawn to thick woods and wide fields.

Brenda sighed enviously. 'This is a beautiful place,' she said, sinking deeply into the soft cushions of the settee.

Anna Selassie smiled. 'It is, isn't it? I'm very happy here. This house has such a welcoming, contented aura about it. I felt that the very first time I stepped in the door. Coffee?'

'Thank you – no sugar. Are you an artist as well as a potter?' Brenda asked.

'I do landscapes, and sea-scapes, and sky-scapes, and when I want to e-scape from those, yes, I pot,' she replied humorously. 'Or just potter on the beach or sail in Brancaster Harbour. That's one of my pieces.' She pointed to a large bowl on a nearby table.

It weighed heavy in Brenda's hands and still showed faint lines left by the tips of fingers when soft and on the wheel, but the use of brightly coloured, thick swirling glazes gave it a glowing radiance, if you cared for such things. It was a far cry from the delicate brilliance of translucent porcelain.

'Very nice,' Brenda said, carefully replacing it. 'I'm sorry about your brother. It must have come as a shock to you.'

Anna nodded ruefully. 'A complete surprise, and I do grieve for him, of course, but we were not really close, you understand. Arthur was my half-brother. My mother died within six months of my being born. She was my father's first wife. Arthur's mother was his third. He was a Henry, you see, but he didn't quite manage as many wives as Henry VIII. He and his fourth died when I was thirteen, in a foggy pile-up on the M6. Arthur would have been about three or four. Grandad King took both of us in charge then, bless his heart. He had shoe factories in Nottingham, and was very wealthy, so we were well cared for. I went off to school near Brighton. Arthur had a whole string of nannies and nurses until he went to boarding school. Later I went on to study art in London, and Arthur went to Southampton University, and then Cambridge. We kept in touch, but our lives were, well, apart, you might say.'

'Do you know much about his life, then, before he married?' Brenda asked.

'Not really. Like me, he was a bit wild in his early days. He wandered abroad for a while, no doubt womanizing all the time, like my father did, but he could do that – neither of us was ever short of money. Grandad didn't mind, he was the King of Kings, and could bring either of us to heel when he wished to do so. He fixed Arthur up in those laboratories in Cambridge, he had shares in that, and told Arthur when it was time to settle down. I shouldn't think Gwenda was one of his regular women, she was too nice for that. He showed a bit of sense, marrying her. She must be devastated, poor thing, and those two lovely children. I positively doted on them when Gwenda last brought them over.'

'Their marriage had split up recently, did you know that?'

'No, I didn't. That's a shame. Another woman, I suppose. He was off Grandad's leash, of course. The old boy's senile now, and in a home. He didn't even know me when I went to see him last week.'

'Off his leash?'

Anna Selassie shrugged her shoulders. 'We had all the money we needed from Grandad to live well and comfortably – he helped us to buy this place – but the big fortune has yet to come our way, or my way now. Grandad sold the shoe business years ago, and he invested the proceeds wisely. His fortune is left solely to his grandchildren, if we survive him. Well, I mean, it'll all come to me, now Arthur's passed on, that's if I can hang on a bit longer. Grandad could live a fair few years yet, bless him. He's only ninety.'

'Were you aware that your brother had recently received a death-threat letter?'

'No! He and I didn't communicate, you know. It's all very silly really, but when I told him that I was going to marry Matthew, he's an Ethiopian with a liberal dose of Scots blood in him, Arthur got all stroppy about mixed marriages and how I was letting the family down. I told him he could take a running jump and take it or leave it. He left it. I haven't spoken to him since. Funny that, because Matthew's got real royal blood in him, even if some of his ancestors were a murderous lot. Which is better than the pseudo-kingship connections that Arthur and my father were so fanatical about. Arthur was rather – how can I put it? – dogmatically self-centred. If he didn't like a situation or something, he'd just walk away from it, as though it didn't exist.'

There had been the faint sounds of voices in the adjoining room: now there came the clear sound of a violin being tuned, and then some scales, but when that changed into Paganini's twenty-sixth caprice, Brenda's head jerked to one side in surprise, as if that new position allowed her to hear better.

'That's beautiful playing,' she breathed, as much to herself as to her host. 'Your husband?'

Anna Selassie smiled and shook her head. 'Matthew only makes violins. That's Isaac – what's his name? – playing. Many

93

of the top violinists come here for practise instruments or ones for their pupils or protégés, and they often buy. Matthew has the Stradivari touch, you see, and a good new instrument with potential is often better value than one that's merely old.'

'That's Stern playing?' Brenda said, eyebrows raised.

Anna chuckled happily. 'If you say so. It sounds rather lovely to me.'

Robin Redhead had a thick mop of shiny black hair and a face with rather crumpled features which formed a permanently dissatisfied expression. However, although he was on the short side, he was lean and muscular and obviously full of energy, since his track-suited body fidgeted restlessly at being confined, even for a moment, to the restrictions of a chair.

'You were one of Arthur King's closest friends, at university and after, I believe,' Reg Finch stated, looking curiously round the gymnasium of the school near Newmarket.

'I suppose I was – once,' Redhead replied curtly while flexing the fingers of his right hand.

'Oh, there was a rift, was there?' Reg asked.

'You could say that.'

'What caused the rift?'

'Gwenda Killibury was my girl-friend. I should have known better than let her meet him, but I really didn't think she was his type. He turned on the charm act, and like a fool, she fell for it.' He shrugged his shoulders. 'They all did, one way or another. If his patter didn't get them to roll on their backs for him straight away, he'd use his more serious line, about how it was time he settled down; then he'd tell them about his Grandad's millions. That usually did the trick.'

'But King did marry Gwenda Killibury. Is that what you were planning to do?' Reg inquired, watching the other's mobile face intently.

'I wanted to, but our relationship hadn't developed that far by then.'

'So you had a row? Was it a verbal row, or did it get physical?'

Redhead frowned. 'Verbal. You didn't pick a fight with Arthur, not when you knew him. He was bigger and had a longer reach than me, besides, he'd done his self-defence and could look after himself. He needed to. He was bound to come up against opposition when he set out to pull men's birds as he did; but not from me. I can't remember how the row started, but I know I told him if he didn't leave Gwenda alone I'd shove his bloody sword Excalibur right down his throat. He just laughed and said why didn't I try it. I haven't seen him since. That must be four, nearly five years ago. I was surprised when you phoned and wanted to talk to me. I know nothing about his latest goings-on, but you can't tell me that he left other women alone when he married Gwenda. Well, you can, but I won't believe you. There were dozens of girls before her, some serious – they got hurt emotionally, others were just having a good time. No! There's no way I can remember all their names. Not after all these years.'

9

'Yes, I remember that old house down Badon Lane quite well, Inspector,' Willie O'Connor said, puckering up his forehead thoughtfully, and at the same time scratching his left ear with a long bony finger. 'It ain't that long ago we finished it. Funny bloke, that King chap. Very positive, he was, about what he wanted – most of the time – then he'd change his mind about silly little things, almost as though he was doing it for the sheer hell of it, just to mess us about. Well,' he shrugged his lean shoulders while the bony finger rubbed this time at his beak of a nose, 'we builders get used to that sort of thing, though it's mainly the women we have trouble with, anything over and above the original quote gets charged as extras, at day work rates, and there was a fair old bit ended up on his bill. Still, he paid up, and you can't ask more than that, can you?'

'We'll want copies of all your quotes, drawings, sketches and paperwork, for our files,' Walsh explained, leaning forward to pick up one of the blueprint-sized plans from the builder's untidy desk.

'No problem. I'll get my girl doing copies this afternoon when she comes in. She's part-time, you see. That's the ground-floor plan you've got there. Giles, the architect, did that. We pretty well gutted the place, downstairs, at any rate. Early Victorian – slate damp course, that was all right really, but we drilled and pressure-impregnated another, to be on the safe side. The worm had got into a lot of the woodwork downstairs, so that all had to go, and there was a bit of movement with the wall foundations, there usually is, but it weren't serious. Still, we dug it all out nice and deep and locked the whole lot solid in concrete. All the inside and a good three feet round the outside, tied with steel reinforcing bars. That won't move now, not in a million years.'

'Solid floors? I thought I noticed air-bricks?' Walsh commented.

'S'right, that was one of his changes. Initially he was going to have solid floors with thermoplastic tiles, but at the last minute, just as we we was going to pour the concrete, he decided he wanted wooden ones. So we dropped our levels inside, and that's what he had. The customer's always right – while he has his cheque book handy. I didn't care. Work's not so easy to find just now, so the longer that job went on the better it was for me – besides, it made the wiring and plumbing easier.'

'How high was the floor above the concrete? Did you leave any access to that space?'

Willie O'Connor looked thoughtful. 'Four by two timbers on pillar walls three bricks high. About twelve inches, and, as I say, there's pipes and wiring in that space. The only access is to the radiator drain cocks via screwed-down floor-boards, but you wouldn't be able to move about down there, if that's what you mean, even if you could wriggle down, because of the pillar walls. They're solid on the concrete.'

'There was a small brass bolt and a shed-type panel lock fitted to the sitting-room door; the mortice lock had been removed. Did you do that?'

O'Connor blinked in surprise and shook his head. 'What the devil did he do that for? They were the original doors, they were. They had loads of coats of paint on them, but we had them stripped and sanded by an old fellow out Barton way. Only old pine, of course, but they came up lovely, they did, with three coats of varnish on them. Nothing wrong with the lock, either, after we'd cleaned and oiled it.'

'I see,' Walsh murmured. 'Was there anything about the job that was strange or out of the ordinary?'

O'Connor's bony face grimaced almost into a sneer. Clearly he thought Walsh's questions had drifted from the sublime to the ridiculous. 'Well,' he said impatiently, 'when we dug out the kitchen floor we found an old well, which we filled in with rubbish, and under the sitting-room we found the remains of a brick floor from an older building. It may have been a stable once. Then there were the bones . . .'

'Bones?'

'S'right. I weren't there myself when they found them. A couple of feet or so down, near the side door. The lads thought they were human, so they got one of your coppers out, and then they sat around wasting time that I had to pay for. If they'd dug down a bit more they'd have found the skull. They weren't human bones at all, they was dog bones, but it were a bloody great big dog, all the same.'

He was surprised by the sudden look of intense irritation on the Chief Inspector's face, but he shrugged his shoulders phlegmatically. If you ask silly questions . . .

The estate to the west of the city had been built perhaps two or three years ago. Certainly not long enough for the stumpy bare trees and shrubs in the gardens to have given the site some character.

Brenda Phipps rang the door bell of Number 3, Docking Drive, then stood back from the glass-panelled door.

The woman who eventually appeared was tall and thin, wearing a shapeless black dress of a loose woollen material that looked none too clean. She had a short, pinched nose, tinted wire-framed spectacles and long crinkly black hair. 'Yes?' she said, suspiciously.

'I'd like to have a word with Mr Mark Ambrose, if he's at home,' Brenda stated brightly.

'Well, you can't, because he isn't.'

Brenda looked at her watch. 'Oh. I thought he'd be home by now. He is a schoolteacher, isn't he?'

'What do you want to know for? Who are you, anyway?' The woman's voice became aggressive.

'I'm a police officer,' Brenda explained in a matter-of-fact voice. 'I just want to have –' But that was as far as she got.

The woman, presumably Mrs Ambrose, suddenly behaved as though she was being attacked by a horde of wasps. Her arms waved wildly, but from her mouth flooded a stream of words, some of which, although in common usage, in the overall context of the others became foul expletives. The tirade continued, even after the door had been slammed shut.

Brenda shrugged her shoulders and turned away. The woman was a throwback to the anti-everything activists of the sixties but Brenda's business was not with her. She could arrange a meeting with Mark Ambrose on neutral ground, at his school perhaps.

In the mean time she had others to go and see. There was Gerald Sinclair, the second of the local animal rights activists that Dr Julian Fry, the computer expert, had given her, and Elizabeth Asher, the receptionist at the place where King had worked. After that, if there was still time, she would also see Dr Anita Grant, the woman who Gwenda King claimed was having an affair with her husband.

Jim MacDunn had installed the alarm system in Glein House down Badon Lane. He lived south of Cambridge, in a modern maisonette incongruously appended, with a dozen others, to a little rural village near Royston.

MacDunn had some of the Celtic features often seen in those born in the Highlands of Scotland – thinning reddish-fair hair, intelligent close-set blue eyes, and a stubby nose on a round, freckled, attractively ugly face, but instead of being a muscular six foot plus, MacDunn was weedy and thin, and barely five feet seven.

'I moved down here from Edinburgh last August,' he explained, his voice soft and lilting, 'but I've been with the same firm since I left school. My wife went off with this other fellow, you see, and well, when the chance came to transfer down here and make a new start, I jumped at it. I like it here. I've made some friends and I'm always busy.'

'You worked on the Glein House system from the beginning, I believe?' Walsh asked.

MacDunn nodded. 'The initial inquiry went to our head office in London, but they passed it on to me. I first saw Dr King . . . let me see . . .' He thumbed through his diary. 'October, last year. I got the drawings of the new place he was buying, and the general outline of what he wanted the system to do. Yes, that's right, the local Crime Prevention man had given him some suggestions. Anyway, from those I drew up some layout plans for head office to price up for the quote.'

'So you do the lot? Plan it, install it and test it?'

MacDunn nodded. 'The only thing I can't do properly is to program the computer, at least, not the one in the Fort Knox control box. I'm going to evening classes, but I don't find it easy. So head office do that. As for the testing, that needs two. The area manager usually comes down to do it with me. It's the company's rules that the final testing is done by someone other than the installer, for obvious reasons.'

'So you fit the sensors and contact breakers in place, then run the wiring to the control box. Were the builders still working?' Walsh asked.

MacDunn smiled the smile of the expert technician. 'Noo,' he drawled patiently. 'First I run the wiring through the steel trunking to the sockets in the control box casing. I don't fit the sensors until the builders are finished banging about, and the main control panel, the expensive bit, goes in last of all. That slots into the casing, and I lock the screws with a little lead seal that's personal to me.'

'So while the builders and decorators were still working,

there were no sensors fitted and the control box wasn't installed? So they couldn't have tampered with the system?' Walsh asked.

MacDunn shook his head. 'Even if they'd altered the wiring or damaged it, I'd have found that out when they'd gone. I check each sensor back to its contact in the control box casing when I actually fit it.'

'So all the sensor things are in place and working before the computer gets put into place?'

'That's right. That's the most valuable bit. I've got a similar one here for a system I'm installing in Bedford. Do you want to see it?' MacDunn asked.

'Yes, why not?'

'There we are,' MacDunn said, using a knife to cut through the thick heat-sealed plastic bubble packaging. 'All I have to do is push these plugs into the sockets in the casing. That's the power one, this is for the videos, that's for the window contact breakers, and so on. Then we feed in the computer program. That's on the cassette head office sends me, and goes in there, and we're ready to go.'

'That's the computer, is it?' Walsh pointed to a black box on the back of the panel.

'No, they're the standby batteries. Once I've plugged the power in and they've charged up, they'll hold the program and operate the system for several hours if there's a mains power-cut. That other box is the computer. This is a 500K memory, so it's pretty powerful, but we can add to that if necessary. It's a very versatile system. Yes, when that's in place and everything's rechecked, it's ready to hand over to the owner. Once he's tapped in his private password number on to the keyboard,' he pointed to the series of buttons on the front of the panel that looked rather like those on a modern telephone, 'which for obvious reasons we don't want to know, the system and the program are locked together, and can't be changed. Any messing about would set the alarm off.'

'And that number sequence has to be tapped in whenever the owner comes in or goes out?'

'That's right. That's the only way the computer will know

who's boss, and who to obey. Anyone unlocking the side door breaks the circuit, but if that secret number's not tapped in within ninety seconds, the computer treats it as an illegal entry, and the alarm goes off,' MacDunn replied, and, as if to emphasize the point, the telephone rang.

Walsh glanced round the room. It was clean and comfortably furnished, but it needed the deft touch of a woman to break up the plain mute colours with bright scatter cushions or pictures on the wall.

Obviously, Walsh deduced, MacDunn lived on his own.

It therefore came as a surprise, a moment later, to hear MacDunn saying, 'Well, no. She's not here. Yes, but I don't know what time. Can I give her a message?'

Not all Sherlock Holmes-type deductions hit the nail right on the head, Walsh acknowledged to himself, and looked round more closely for such signs as a woman in residence might leave. He found one not far away from where he was sitting. On the floor, by a small bureau, was an open work-basket, and lying on the top, with one leg limply hanging over the side, was a thin harlequin rag doll. A threaded needle stuck out of the body's tiny black and white diamond torso. Was it a doll though? His perceptions were not working well this evening. He reached out to pick it up, and found that it was more complex than it at first appeared. It was a puppet, nearly complete and very well made, as far as Walsh could judge.

'I'll get her to ring you back then,' MacDunn said and put the telephone down. 'Sorry about that, Inspector,' he went on. 'When it rings I never know if it might be trouble with an alarm installation or not. Oh! You've found one of Jean's puppets. Good, aren't they?'

'Jean? Your wife?' Walsh asked.

'No, she's my girl-friend. She goes to a sewing circle. Some of them do patchwork quilting, others do embroidery. Jean chose to make puppets. Likes pulling the strings, probably,' he said with a slight smile.

'Does she live here with you?' Walsh asked, unaccountably anxious to confirm his first impressions.

'Sometimes. She's got her own place, of course, but, well,

I'm away a lot of the time and neither of us is sure whether we want to get too tied down,' MacDunn explained. 'Where were we?'

'The lock on the side door? Do you supply it?' Walsh asked.

'We do and we don't,' MacDunn replied. 'We order it, but the lock and keys are sent direct from the supplier to the owner. We set the system up with a lock of our own, then change it for his at the last moment, in his presence, so that we never in fact handle the keys. Otherwise if anyone did break in later, we'd be the first on the suspect list.'

'How difficult would it be to get a duplicate key cut if you did manage to get hold of an original?'

'Not as easy as you'd think, not for a private individual. You can't go to any common or garden key cutter. The people who make the best locks know how tight security is on their keys, and they're very careful about who they sell their key blanks to. Their agents would want some form of identification. An official order, if it was a firm, or the lock's registration card, if it was a private individual, and before you ask, yes, it would be possible for a skilled toolmaker with the right tools to make a copy, but without a blank, that's not an easy job.'

'So you think you safeguard yourself by having an independent tester, by not knowing the secret password and by not having access to the important door lock key, do you?'

'That's the general idea. It's company policy, but I'll tell you this, our head office are very worried about this Dr King installation, and I've been told to give you all the help I can. Even so, we've had the system rechecked by independent consultants, and they can't find anything wrong with it.'

Walsh nodded. Packstone and his Forensic team were having the same problem. 'The control box in King's house, was it still sealed in its plastic bag, like this one was?'

MacDunn nodded. 'Yes, I'm sure it was.'

'Where were you, the evening before last? I have to ask, you understand,' Walsh said.

'Bury St Edmunds,' MacDunn replied promptly, having

anticipated the question, for he handed Walsh a piece of paper with an address written on it. 'A fault developed in a factory installation. I was there from seven o'clock until nearly one in the morning sorting it all out. The manager will confirm that. He wasn't too happy about having his evening messed up either, so he's sure to remember me.'

'Did you install a system in the house of a Dr Parkinson, using this type of control box?' Walsh asked. 'He lives in the Newnham area of Cambridge.'

'I didn't. That was before my time. The name's on my records, of course, but I've not met him.'

Walsh got up. 'Thank you. That'll do, for now.'

As Jim MacDunn opened his front door to let Walsh out they were confronted by a short female figure, standing with an arm raised and a key in her hand.

'Ah!' MacDunn said, as they both stepped back to allow her to enter. 'Jean, this is Chief Inspector Walsh, but he's just leaving.'

Walsh found himself gazing at a startlingly attractive face. Her hair was dark and cut short and she had regular features with a pert nose and perfect lips, but those were only minor points noted in a mere fleeting glance, for it was her eyes that dominated her face and drew his attention. Beautiful, large, dark blue expressive eyes that flashed momentarily with all the emotions of interest, humour, curiosity and challenge.

Eyes like that meant trouble. Eyes like that could reduce strong and confident men to foolish gibbering, for it wasn't just a face that had launched a thousand Greek ships three millennia ago, but the face's eyes – eyes like that. The safest thing to do was to look away, but the coward's way wasn't ever Walsh's way. Age, and a happy marriage, gave him some protection now.

'Pleased to meet you,' Walsh smiled, as he went out of the door and on his way to his car.

The last expressions he saw in those lovely eyes were of puzzlement and annoyance, no doubt because their power had been confronted.

That was a victory to set off against previous losses.

'Arthur King was no worse than most men, I suppose,' Elizabeth Asher, the stout laboratory secretary, said reluctantly, and with a good deal of undisguised bitterness.

Brenda Phipps flipped back an unruly lock of hair from her forehead and looked again round the sitting-room. It was bland, there was no other suitable word for it. It contained a few nice things; that ruby glass vase looked genuinely old, but it was fairly obvious they were accidents in the midst of an accumulation of tat. The best one could say was that nothing in the colour scheme actually clashed, but then nothing really went together either.

There was a pretty clear indication that this woman was anti-men, and that was a pity. One might have expected a secretary to be a mine of gossip and information, with a whole host of anecdotes about the dead man and his relationships with his laboratory work colleagues, but all Brenda had obtained so far were meaningless cliché phrases. It was the bitterness in the voice that was most concerning.

Elizabeth Asher was older than she looked, the faint facial lines round the eyes betrayed that, but there was a regularity about her features that made her, if not exactly pretty, certainly not repellently ugly. What might have occurred for her to so dislike men? Failed relationships probably. Maybe, like many, she'd set her sights too high, only wanting those men who didn't want her. She was too old and plain for King to have made passes at her.

Brenda sighed. She'd rather interview men, her own sex were much more complicated.

'You don't like men?' Brenda posed the question bluntly; that was often the best way.

'No way. I've had more than a basinful of them. I'm independent now. I've got this place of my own, and I don't need them. No man's going to dominate me again,' she replied, more emphatically than she needed.

'Was Arthur King more than usually interested in other women, do you think, even though he was married?' Brenda asked. This woman obviously had the dreaded 'domination' syndrome.

'He'd have gone after anything in skirts, like all of them,' came the reply.

Brenda frowned, another cliché answer. She was learning nothing new about the dead man, but those reddened eyes suggested his death had had some sort of effect on her. Maybe she imagined her own life was threatened as well, but perhaps she just didn't like being interviewed by the police.

'How do you get on with the people at the lab? Do you like working there?'

'It's no worse than other places, if you like being a dogsbody, at everyone's beck and call. Do this, do that, "It must be in the post tonight, and we've run out of toilet rolls, Mrs Asher. Nip out and get some more, and get me a birthday card for the wife, a new pair of socks, some leads for my pencil, and fill my car up with petrol while you're about it,"' Asher moaned. 'They treat me like a skivvy, but I've got to smile and say yes. There aren't many jobs about, and I've still got the mortgage to find each month.'

'Did King ever row with any of the people there?'

'They snap at each other all the time. Nasty lot they are. I didn't get involved, but I know there was trouble between Dr Parkinson and King. I know because I had to type some letters. One of the biggest shareholders was putting pressure on the board to get rid of Dr Parkinson as managing director. Dr Parkinson was convinced that Arthur King was behind it, and that King hoped to get the job instead. That was a few months ago, but nothing came of it. I don't know what happened in the end, except that nothing changed.'

'I see,' Brenda said thoughtfully. 'Now this Dr Anita Grant, where you work – it's been suggested that she'd been having an affair with King. Is that likely?'

'Definitely. Been going on for years. She's a bitch. She

reckons she can get any man she wants, whenever she snaps her fingers. She'll get her come-uppance one of these days.'

Brenda rose to her feet. More clichés, it was a waste of time talking to her at the moment. 'One last question, and I'm sure you understand why I must ask it. Where were you the evening Dr Arthur King died?'

Elizabeth Asher flung her hands in the air angrily. 'That's great, that is. Do you really think a mere woman like me could kill a strong man like him? Where was I? Well, I'll tell you where I was all evening. I was baby-sitting an old lady, three doors down, so her daughter could have an evening out. Number 112. Go and ask her. She got back about eleven.'

'Thank you for your help,' Brenda said calmly. 'If you think of anything that might be useful to our inquiries, please get in touch.'

Elizabeth Asher needed a friend whose shoulder she could cry on. There seemed to be a lot of mixed-up emotions in her that needed sorting out. Maybe that friend was the person on the telephone which started to ring as Brenda left the flat.

'It's terrible news, Sergeant Finch. To think that one of our number has died so suddenly, and in suspicious circumstances, too,' the grey-haired old vicar said sadly, yet giving the impression that the disastrous event might give fuel to many an evening's conversation. 'But I don't really think there's much that I can tell you to help your investigations. We limit our Arthurian Society to only twelve members. Not because there were only twelve knights round Arthur's table, but simply because more than that's too many. We meet for dinner once a month, you see. Sometimes we have a speaker, but not always, and we just eat well, and enjoy our own company and conversation. Arthur was, well, very enthusiastic. With a name like his, that's quite understandable. He was rather dogmatic, and occasionally, well, he did start arguments, which isn't quite the thing, is it? A discussion's all very well, but it spoils it if you take things too seriously. I gave you our list of present members, didn't I? We'll have to elect another now that Arthur's gone to pastures new, so to speak, but we've always got a waiting list. Yes, well, anything to do with King Arthur is quite acceptable, it's such a wonderful period in our history, isn't it? Dear me, the sword had Excalibur on it, did it? How interesting. The others will find this all most fascinating. Don't go just yet, let me answer that telephone, then you can tell me more.'

10

The street lights of Newnham Road glowed a hazy yellow in the murky evening mist, but the park and recreational ground of Lammas Land, which bordered its eastern side and stretched down to the river Cam, lay bleak, dark and deserted.

As the lone grey car turned into the narrow lane opposite Barton Road, a dark figure stepped out from the shadows of a high wall, and waved an arm.

The car window was wound down. 'I thought we were meeting down the end there,' the driver said irritably.

'We are. I was early, so I walked up to meet you,' the dark figure replied calmly, opening the back door and climbing in behind the driver.

The car drove on down the lane.

'Why have we got to meet here of all places? I'm really worried. I've had the police round,' the driver went on with head half turned to make the words audible in the back.

'Watch where you're going. Here's the paddling pool on the left. The car-park's just a bit further on, on the right. Take it easy, there's a big pot-hole just inside. I'm parked over near the far corner, by the river.'

'I still don't see why we couldn't meet somewhere better than this place,' the driver grumbled as the car was steered through the gap in the hedge, which was the entrance to the unlit car-park, then bumped its way round the other vehicles, across the uneven stony gravelled surface, to the far corner.

The darkness and silence closed in on them both when the engine had been switched off and the car lights had faded.

'You've had the police round, have you? What did you tell them?' the figure asked, leaning forward.

'Nothing. They didn't ask about that, but they're bound to come back. What then? I still don't understand why you wanted –'

'Don't worry. The police will ask you no more questions. I promise you,' the figure interrupted, suddenly slipping the loop of five amp plastic-covered electrical flex over the driver's head and quickly pulling it tight round the other's bare exposed neck.

There was a distinct pleasure in realizing how clever one had been to tie the little wooden toggles on each end of the wire. They were so easy to grip and didn't hurt one's hands. With a knee pushing on the back of the front seat, all one had to do was pull, and pull and pull. Those croaky noises the other was making sounded really funny. You had to laugh too. 'No more questions', that was the funniest clever joke ever. If piano or E string wire had been used instead of flex, that head would have been sliced right off by now, like a piece of cheese . . . a piece of cheese.

It hurt to laugh so much. Why did one's heartbeats throb and pound so loud in one's ears? Pull, keep pulling. Why were these hands and arms trembling like this?

There had been so many unexpected interruptions during the evening that Dr Anita Grant had to hurry to complete her preparations for John Bailey's visit, ostensibly arranged to discuss what action those who worked at the laboratory could take against the animal rights activists who had probably killed their former colleague, Arthur King.

That policewoman – detective constable or whatever she called herself – had wasted a great deal of time with her persistent questioning about poor old Arthur's family relationships, how he got on with those at work, animal rights threats, then lastly, coming like a bombshell to make all her neutral answers sound quite ludicrous, who did she think might have sent the anonymous note telling King's wife that there had been a long-standing affair between herself and King. That had really rocked her on her heels and it had been some moments before her agile mind had come up with a suitable reply. It had seemed pointless to deny it outright, so she settled for it having been a recent, casual affair. The woman detective's face had remained so impassive that it had been difficult to judge whether she was being believed or not. Fortunately a telephone call had interrupted them, and that had given her a chance to sort her thoughts out. She had been better composed for the rest of the interview, particularly for the question of where she had been the night Arthur had died. It was useful having a wide group of women friends, and meeting them regularly. It was an unwritten rule amongst them, especially for those who were married, that an alibi would be provided on demand and without question, but whether the police would check that sort of thing out in detail was another matter; probably they wouldn't.

That had taken some of the evening, but there had been other things needing to be done before she could relax her tensions away in a hot bath.

Now her body was clean and sweet-smelling, and completely naked under her short towelling dressing gown. That would allow for a little deliberate accidental exposure, if it proved necessary to rouse her visitor's ardour.

After she'd hurried to get all that done, however, John Bailey was late.

Anita wanted this new relationship to get off to a good start, so she needed to curb that natural instinct of hers to dominate, or try to. It hadn't bothered Arthur, his ego had been so strong that anything abrasive she might have said just bounced off his protective shield like water off a duck's back, but John, although he thought himself so clever, was much less mature, and would react differently.

Then the bell rang.

Anita rose to her feet and went to open the door.

'Well!' she said. 'This is a fine time to turn up. I was just going to bed, but now you're here, you might as well come in.' Those were not the words she had planned to use and she looked anxiously up at his face to see what his reaction was.

There was a wild, strained, almost mad look on John Bailey's face, and his eyes glowed fearsomely.

Anita gave a gasp of fright and stepped back in alarm, but she was not quick enough. He had kicked the door shut and darted forward, reaching out with both arms to grab her. Then she was wrenched against his body so violently that her breath was forced from her lungs. There was no air left to scream, but she couldn't anyway, for his mouth was pressing down on hers so hard that it that felt as though her lips were being split against her teeth. She struggled in sheer panic, writhing and twisting, trying to break his hold and release the suffocating pressure on her face. Her head was already swimming from lack of oxygen and she made one last all-out effort to break free, but he was far too strong for her. Instead, his arms tightened their grip, forcing her to bend backwards until only her toes touched the floor. The thought flashed through her mind that there was no need to rouse his passion, that was patently and painfully obvious. She was utterly helpless and soon could struggle no more. Her body went limp, seemingly becoming detached from her mind. As if in a dream she felt the towelling robe being wrenched from her, and then she was flung cruelly to the floor.

The mauling and squeezing of her soft tender flesh that followed was only numbly painful, but then, suddenly, he really did hurt her. That forced a cry of pain from between her bruised lips. That pain, however, had a strange effect on her; somehow it stimulated sensations within her that had been deadened by shock and fear. Now her body started to move and do things of its own volition. At first it was just to improve and vary the feelings of what was happening to her, but then the movements became more active and urgent. Her mind was furiously angry that her body should co-operate on its own or do anything to prolong this outrage of her person, but that all suddenly dissipated as she burst into a frantic wild

110

delirium of her own all-embracing passion. Her nails dug deep into Bailey's back as she writhed and screamed and moaned. Wave after wave of overwhelming sensations flashed through her body like the ear-shattering explosions of thunder from an approaching storm, until a last terrifying crescendo left her utterly exhausted and bewildered.

As she lay there panting, a small voice in her brain warned her to be careful, that this man was unpredictable and dangerous, and that it would be wise to be extra careful with what she said. Yet the words that passed her sore lips when she'd regained enough breath risked everything.

'You bastard. You bloody bastard. You raped me,' she croaked hoarsely.

John Bailey's florid face forced a death's-head grin, but his words were slurred and almost incoherent. 'Did I hell! You got just what you wanted. You've been prowling round the lab lately like a frustrated old hen. I really needed that, too. You're a right little mad-cap when you get going, aren't you? Is my back bleeding? It feels like it. You ought to cut your damned fingernails.'

Anita pushed herself to her knees, still breathing heavily, and surprised herself by feeling proud to see the scratches her fingernails had left. 'Yes it is, and it serves you bloody well right. That was no way to treat a lady.'

'A lady? I thought I was grappling with a dozen tigresses on heat.'

Anita smiled – it was difficult, with those waves of contentment still rippling through her body, to do otherwise – but she shook her head.

It looked as though she'd found a more than suitable replacement for Arthur King, if she could control him. His violent approach had taken her by surprise, but it had ended up as an exhilarating experience. Next time she would be ready and able to give as good as she got, right from the beginning. That was something to look forward to, but now she felt sweaty and hot. She went to the bathroom for towels, turned up the heating, and made coffee, liberally lacing it with brandy.

John Bailey still lay on the floor, propped up on one elbow

watching her movements, shamelessly staring at her most intimate areas. She made no attempt to cover herself; on the contrary, she sat cross-legged before him and eyed his nakedness with as much interest as he was displaying toward hers.

'We were supposed to meet to talk about what we might do about these animal rights threats, John,' she murmured, sipping from her cup. He was lean and muscular and well endowed, there, leaning against her settee, flexing the fingers of his hands and staring at them as though puzzled by his ability to move them as he did.

'Yes,' he replied, his eyes regaining some of their earlier wildness. 'We've got to give those buggers something to think about, and I know how to do it, too. It'll scare the pants off them but do no real harm. I could do it on my own but it'd be better if you drove the car.'

'Sure,' she said, gently running the tips of her fingers on the inside of his thigh. She felt light-headed and rash, much as she often had done in her wild student days, and the mellow fumes of the brandy heightened the rag-day feeling of recklessness.

So it was that at two o'clock in the morning, now dressed in a thick sweater and jeans, Anita, with her head still in white woolly irrational clouds, slid herself behind the wheel of Bailey's dark green Morgan.

She glanced at her companion before she slowly let up the clutch. His jaw was firmly gritted and strangely he was again staring at his hands, and flexing his fingers. The momentary feeling of doubt and fear at what she was doing and who she was with became swamped by the sensual exhilaration caused by the powerful car's acceleration.

'Right, pull in here, and keep the engine running,' John Bailey whispered, excitement again slurring his words. 'I won't be a minute.'

Bailey ran lightly along the road, glancing at the house numbers until he found the one he wanted. He tiptoed up the front path. The little plastic bag of petrol in his hand was sealed tightly at the top with an elastic band. His fingers nervously pulled that off, then he eased the bag carefully through the letter box and let it drop. He heard a muffled thud as it hit the floor inside. Then he lit a cigarette, drew on it hard so that it glowed brightly, and pushed that through the letter box as well. There was an instant whoosh as the vapour inside ignited, then Bailey sprinted back to his car and leapt inside.

'Get moving,' he panted.

The next part of the plan was to phone for the fire brigade, but the first phone box was out of order, and it was another six minutes before his message was snapped out to the 999 operator and another twelve minutes before the first appliance arrived.

In the mean time the fire had taken a hold, spreading with consummate ease through the open doors of the downstairs rooms, and soon flames were roaring up the stairway to the landing above; but it was the smoke and fumes from the foam-packed furniture which presented the greatest danger.

The two dazed and panic-stricken adults escaped eventually by breaking their bedroom window and jumping to the ground, unable, because of the intensity of the flames and smoke on the landing, to reach their two children in the front bedroom. However, that was achieved by firemen with breathing apparatus and ladders, from the outside of the house. Very soon two pretty, unconscious little girls, aged four and six, were fighting for their young lives, in the intensive care unit of Addenbrooke's Hospital.

The passage of the river Cam, as it flows through the city and the stately backs of the colleges, can best be described as being gently placid.

However, at one point in its journey, there is a significant sudden drop in levels. Only eight or ten feet, and not particularly spectacular, but enough to warrant, in earlier times, a water mill.

There is no mill there today, but the power potential is still apparent, especially after heavy rains, then the water does roar over the fall and under the bridge, to swirl and eddy in the dark pool beneath.

Such natural bounty is now an insignificant energy source: no doubt a learned economist would explain why. Yet those earlier ages had their economists too, with different assessments of values. Someone, rumour has him to be an ex-barefist boxer, once calculated that there was enough flow of water in the river to drive not just one mill, but two. So he raised the necessary capital, and cut a dike to bring water from about a mile upstream to a new mill, which was built only a few hundred yards away from the first. No doubt the competition benefited the inhabitants of the town.

That narrow cut still exists. It runs quite straight and never very deep, parting the meadow land of Sheep's Green from the manicured recreational grass of Lammas Land, the whole being a favoured area for sunbathers, swimmers and picnickers, particularly in the summer, and used all the year round by dog walkers.

Postman Gordon Bligh was a dog walker.

After a night shift in the sorting office it was good to get out in the early morning mist to stretch his legs before going back home for a light breakfast and then to bed and sleep. There would be no one in the house to disturb his rest, save Ben, his elderly Labrador, but he wouldn't, not if he'd had a good run.

It was a fair walk from where he lived in Newnham, firstly to the old swimming pool and then along the river to the mill bridge and back by the old Mill Cut. There was time to let his mind wander as he ambled along, and plenty to think about. The Post Office was planning thousands of job cuts during the next few years, having at last made their automatic letter-sorting machines work properly. The damned things could read handwritten addresses and post codes as well as, if not better than, the human eye. So now humans could be discarded, cast out like unwanted clothes, and Gordon, at fifty, could apply for voluntary redundancy, if he wanted. The forms were in his pocket. The union man had said that with his years of service it might be worth as much as twenty thousand pounds to him. It was staggeringly tempting. He'd never have the chance to get a lump sum like that again, unless Mr Littlewood looked kindly on one of his weekly pools coupons, but on the other hand there were still fifteen years to go before he got his old age pension. He'd need another job of some sort.

He threw a stick ahead for the dog to chase, but it fell into the water of the Mill Cut. Old Ben wasn't going in after that, no way. It was much too cold a morning for swimming, and wet blankets in his warm basket would take a lot of drying. He looked back reproachfully at his master. Gordon Bligh pretended to be unaware of the dog's reproof, and instead looked at the stick, drifting slowly towards him on the dark sluggish water, and that was why he saw the body.

The part nearest him, yet well out of reach, was only a dark bundle of cloth protruding a few inches above the surface, and smoothly rounded, as though air was trapped within the material. The rest was an eerie whitish form, one moment appearing to be legs, the next, a mere trick of the light, but what could be identified with certainty was a half-clenched hand, brought to the surface by a patch of thick weed, which also seemed to be anchoring the body.

There could be no mistake, however many times he blinked and stared and rubbed his eyes.

Redundancy and water mills were a long way from his mind as he ran back home, to pant a gasping call to the police station.

By seven o'clock the area by the Mill Cut buzzed with uniformed people, and white tapes on sticks restricted public access. A few others in plain clothes congregated in the small, roughly surfaced car-park near the children's paddling pool.

'It's getting a bit of a habit, this early morning stuff,' Dr Richard Packstone said drily, watching his staff search the scrubby undergrowth that edged the stream.

'There's nothing to identify her, I believe, but you've found some of her lower clothing?' Walsh asked, looking regretfully at the number of people now treading the soft areas that might have told him a story, had he been free to get on his hands and knees and do some tracking. Their video records were all very well, but they were a two-dimensional, sterile world. There was nothing like the real thing, and doing it oneself.

'Yes, underclothes, in the corner, by that grey car over there. The woman must have been out walking on her own last night and got waylaid by a prowler who was waiting for just such an opportunity. It looks as if she was dragged over there into the bushes, that's where the offence probably took place,' Packstone replied coolly.

'That's how it was, you think?' Walsh muttered.

'Very likely. I've seen too many rape cases, but this one's killed afterwards to hide his identity. A vicious, dangerous man, Sydney. You'll need to get him quick or there'll be others.'

'She was strangled, I believe?' Brenda Phipps asked.

'Garrotted rather, but in a strange way. You've seen the body?' Packstone asked.

Walsh nodded. He'd woken very early that morning and not been able to get back to sleep, so he'd been up and ironing shirts and bed sheets when he'd learned of the body's discovery.

'We haven't though, have we, Reg? May we?' Brenda requested.

'Yes, she hasn't been taken away yet.'

The body lay on a stretcher under a white sheet and in a zippered plastic body bag, awaiting transport to the morgue and another autopsy. Packstone bent to expose the face and neck, and pointed to the thin bluish-black line across the throat. 'Possibly something like a piece of electric flex, but it wasn't twisted all the way round her neck, as you'd expect. Perhaps when he'd finished with her he rolled her face down, put the flex round her throat and his knee on the back of the neck, and just pulled.'

'Chief,' Brenda said quietly, reaching out to touch Walsh's arm. 'Her face is familiar, and those little gold studs in her ears. I've seen her recently.'

116

Walsh stared at the bloated distorted features, trying to see them relaxed and in life. 'There is something about her, now I come to think of it.'

'Who did you interview yesterday, Brenda?' Reg asked.

'There was Mark Ambrose's wife, but it certainly isn't her,' Brenda said positively.

'Ambrose?' Packstone yawned loudly. 'There was a bad fire at a house owned by an Ambrose last night, somewhere in the Bar Hill area. The family are lucky to be alive. The Fire Chief reckons it was petrol through the letter box, and he's usually right on that sort of thing, but I'll have to find someone to put on it this morning.'

'Was your Ambrose in Bar Hill, Brenda?' Walsh asked.

'Yes, Number 3, Docking Drive, then I went to Girton to see a Sinclair, but he was on his own, there were no women there. After that I saw Elizabeth Asher, the secretary at the laboratory where Arthur King worked. She lives in one of those awful barrack-block-type flats in Histon. Then, lastly,' Brenda went on, 'Dr Anita Grant, the woman at the laboratory who King had been having an affair with.'

'Dr Parkinson's secretary, Asher. That's who it probably is. She's the right age and stature,' Walsh said quietly, pulling on his chin thoughtfully.

'Yes, I think so too, Chief,' Brenda confirmed.

Packstone straightened up sharply and swung round. 'Who's got the list of the cars that were here when we arrived?' he called out.

One of the uniformed sergeants came over. 'I've got it, sir. Do you want it?'

'You've found out the names and addresses of all the owners? Is there an Asher?' Walsh asked.

The sergeant looked in his notebook, and nodded. 'That grey four-door Mazda, over in the corner, near where most of the woman's clothes were found.'

Packstone sprang into action. 'Photographers, video men! That grey Mazda!' he shouted as he hurried guiltily away.

Walsh smiled to himself. Richard Packstone was a meticulously efficient man, but here, this morning, he'd summed up the situation wrongly. The skilled men had been set to work on the most obvious areas first, searching for clothing and signs of a struggle. They'd have got round to the cars in due course, but later. They'd had no reason to suspect a link with a previous murder.

'Well, her killer probably doesn't live within walking distance, boss,' Reg Finch suggested. 'Or else he'd have driven her car away and dumped it somewhere else.'

'Not necessarily. If he moved the car he'd still need to get himself back home somehow – besides, our friend from the lab, Dr Parkinson, lives near here. He's the first we'll check out,' Walsh replied.

'You think she had an assignment with some man who planned to kill her?' Brenda queried. 'But why come to a spot like this? She was her own woman, with her own flat. If she wanted to meet Parkinson or any man, she could do it at her home in comfort; but I don't think that's right anyway. Last night I got the distinct impression that she'd got it in for men in general. Yes, now I remember, her phone started ringing as I left. It might be worth –'

'We'll go out to her flat in a little while,' Walsh interrupted, 'but we'll wait for Packstone to check her car first. If she drove it here, maybe her keys are in it, and they'll save us a bit of trouble getting in.'

However, there were no keys, and no handbag, either inside the car or outside, but there was an explanation for the unusual feature that had puzzled Packstone.

'She was strangled while she sat in the front seat,' he explained, 'by someone in the back. The ligature, flex, or whatever it was must have been dropped over her head and then pulled tight. You can still see the indentations it left on the sides of the front seat head-rest. I'm wondering whether she was sexually assaulted at all, or whether her clothes were torn off just to make us think so.'

'Maybe her killer didn't want to be seen near her flat,' Brenda suggested. 'So he arranged a meeting at the first lonely spot he could think of. Why didn't he –'

'You're speculating and jumping to conclusions before

we've got all the facts, Brenda,' Walsh remarked drily. 'He probably took her keys and sneaked into her flat later, to make sure she hadn't left anything to incriminate him. We'll go and see if he was successful.'

His reasoning was just as speculative, but since the general purpose was practical and logical, neither of the others could be bothered to point that out.

'Richard,' Walsh called out, 'we'll still have our meeting on the Arthur King case later this morning, won't we? And may I borrow one of your locksmith chaps to let us into Asher's flat? It'd be handy if he can do fingerprints as well.'

11

'You must be joking. I can't believe it,' Walsh exclaimed, his face expressing his utter surprise and bewilderment.

'Please yourself,' Richard Packstone snapped angrily. 'But I'll say it again, just to make sure there's no misunderstanding. The alarm system in Arthur King's house works perfectly. The placing of the sensors, the sensors themselves, the wiring, the control boxes, the computer and its program have been checked and rechecked by independent experts. They all categorically agree that everything works perfectly now, and that it must have been doing so on the night King died, and what is more, they are prepared to testify to that effect in court, if the need arises. I assure you, they've checked everything with the most sophisticated equipment. There's no possible room for doubt.'

'I didn't mean I doubted your word, Richard,' Walsh explained, still shaking his head. 'But I was relying on you. I was so sure you'd find some technical fault, some way in. Hell's fire, in effect you're saying that King wasn't murdered, because no one could possibly get in or out. Yet the pathologist is stating equally positively that he definitely was murdered, because the way he died could not have been self-inflicted.

119

Where the blazes does that leave us? Between the devil and the deep blue sea.'

'Hardly, boss,' Reg Finch chipped in. 'King's death is a fact. The coroner's not interested in alarm systems, and if no one disputes the pathologist's report, he'll have to bring in a verdict of unlawful killing, and we'll have to investigate it.'

'I know that, Reg,' Walsh snapped angrily, 'but what chance have we got of getting a conviction, even if we find the killer, when our own Forensic people are prepared to swear blind he couldn't have done it, because he couldn't get in? I've never known a situation like this before.'

'But the side door video camera didn't record the dog. How do the experts explain that?' Reg asked.

'They don't. That camera works and operates perfectly now and there's no indication that it ever had an intermittent fault either.'

'So the dog's prints weren't really there, because the camera didn't see it. That's a great deal of help! I suppose you've checked the house for hidden secret entrances, priest holes and the like?' Brenda asked sarcastically.

'They don't exist, Brenda. Of course we've checked – every inch of the place,' Packstone replied gloomily, 'and even if there had been, the alarm system would have been activated, purely by someone being there. I can't explain the dog. I just can't.'

'I gather you've found no unidentified fingerprints, but what about other surface traces, hairs, fluff and so on? Is there anything there to indicate the presence of an intruder?' Reg wanted to know.

Packstone shook his head. 'The carpets were all brand new. Ninety-nine per cent of what the vacuums took up was fluff from those. There are unidentified traces, linen fibres, wool fibres, of course; most will have come from the curtains, cushions, bed sheets and blankets. It'd take months to sort all that lot out, even if I could spare the people, and I can't. That's low priority work, until you can find a suspect.'

'We've got a few people with good motives on a suspect list. King's wife, Parkinson, his sister and his old university chum,

120

but there's nothing yet to tie any of them to the actual killing,' Walsh muttered despondently.

'Well, I can't help that. I only deal in facts. Maybe something helpful will come from the Asher killing,' Packstone suggested.

'It hasn't so far. There're no strange fingerprints and nothing to help us in her flat. If we don't get some sightings of people acting suspiciously, I don't see us getting any further forward than we are now, frankly. Still, if we want to make progress we'll just have to put our best feet forward and our shoulders to the wheel, all at the same time, won't we?' Brenda suggested, trying to be more cheerful than she felt.

'So, you think Asher's killing and the petrol bombing are linked with King's murder,' the Chief Constable said, leaning forward with his arms on his desk and studying the backs of his massive hands pensively. He wasn't posing a question, but merely summarizing what Walsh had already been saying.

'The only doubt I have is the fact that the petrol bomber, or an accomplice, phoned a warning, so it doesn't seem likely that murder was the intention there, but it's too early to say.'

'Right! What do you plan to do now? You can't dispute what Packstone and his experts say about King's alarm system or what's in the pathologist's report, but there's no doubt though that Asher was murdered – perhaps you'd best concentrate on that,' the CC suggested, staring directly at the rather drawn face of his Detective Chief Inspector.

'Obviously I have to broaden the scope of the inquiry, and that means using more people.'

'How many more? We can't have everything else grind to a standstill. Packstone is already complaining about the work load in his department because of this case, and I can't afford to put work out to other forensic labs unless it's absolutely vital. I'm only just holding to my budgeted spend as it is.'

'Three experienced teams for three or four days should break the back of things. After that, well, it depends what crops up.'

'When will you be ready to brief them?'

'Two o'clock.'

The CC leaned back in his chair and put the tips of his fingers carefully together. 'Good. Now, you don't seem to me your normal perky self, Sidney. Are you all right? You're not sickening for something, are you?'

Walsh smiled bleakly and shook his head. 'We've all had a few disturbed nights lately. No problem there.'

'You'd better get a good night's sleep then. Gwen's still in America, isn't she? When's she due back?'

'Next Thursday.'

'Not long, then. She'll soon sort you out. In the mean time, stop trying to do so much yourself. You should delegate more, I've told you that before. Step back a bit and try and detach yourself from things. If you get too close you never will see the wood for the trees.' He scratched the side of his nose thoughtfully. 'Now, that reminds me of something I wanted to ask you. What the devil's all this about you taking a revolver from that woman doctor, Hammington? She's my wife's doctor. A bit of a weird woman, I've always thought. The duty sergeant said you'd booked it in on the morning King's body was found, without making a report. But he's no fool, he noted that it had just been fired. What's that all about?'

Walsh explained briefly what had happened when he'd followed the dog tracks through the wood.

'Christ, and you haven't done anything about it? What the devil's the matter with you? Why haven't you charged her? Frightened she'd say in court that you were out to rape her because you got randy while your wife was away in the States? You had young Phipps with you, didn't you? Mind you, that don't sound any better, does it? You romping through the woods in the dark with a woman constable. Have you had Hammington checked out? It sounds mighty suspicious, someone with a revolver wandering about near where you've just found a murdered man.'

Walsh nodded. 'Her story's been checked. She was on "call-out" all that night, and her visits tie her time up pretty well,' he muttered, but there was another train of thought going through his mind. The killing of Elizabeth Asher had inexorably drawn some of the attention away from Arthur King's house, to the laboratory where they had both worked. Maybe the answers lay there. On the other hand, perhaps that was what the killer wanted him to think. Was it possible that Elizabeth Asher had been killed merely to throw more confusion into the pot? Why would that be needed after the mind-boggling scenario that had been staged at Glein House, down Badon Lane? There was an airy-fairy mistiness about this whole thing that fitted better the make-believe world of actors and performers, in which the ghostly appearance of Old Shuck could be accepted without question. It was not going to be a simple matter to apply the poultice of cold logic to this problematic wound, and find a healing denominator that could be applied to all events, and make sense of them.

Flurries of rain beat a dismal but soundless patter on the outer of the double-glazed panes of Walsh's office.

Inside, décor-wise, there was little to cheer the critical eye. Pale green walls with a couple of prints, an off-white ceiling, a grey filing cabinet, a double pedestal oak desk and a motley collection of chairs. Faded brown curtains hung by the windows. It was a functional room, a place for those with more practical matters than mere decoration on their minds.

Walsh leaned his elbows on his desk and looked at the faces of those seated opposite. They were interesting characters, some of the brightest team leaders in the constabulary. Having been given a brief résumé of the case they were showing curiously thoughtful expressions while they absorbed what they had heard.

'If this Elizabeth Asher had actually been one of the drug-testing scientists, it would have added to the likelihood of the animal rights extremists having done both killings,' Detective Sergeant Myres observed, in his quiet West Country voice.

'But she wasn't,' Inspector Kennedy interrupted impatiently, 'so it's much more likely that she knew something about King's killer, and had to be silenced permanently. Therefore the chances are that the killer is someone who works at the lab.'

'Possibly,' Detective Constable Ackers said thoughtfully, 'but do you remember that case up in Manchester? A couple of years ago it was. There was a second linked killing in that one. That turned out to be a revenge killing by someone else who was convinced she knew who had done the first murder. Maybe Asher had a grudge against King, and bumped him off, then one of King's lovers, even his wife perhaps, who knew about the grudge, did the "eye for an eye" bit.'

'That's possible,' Brenda Phipps added. 'She certainly had a grudge, although that was against men in general rather than anyone in particular, but I really don't think she had enough up top to put together a package like the one we've got here. As to King's past lovers, we've little to go on since he didn't keep their names in a trophy book. It seems that when he'd finished with them he just forgot about them. We've got a few Christian names, but that's not a lot of help.'

'We're after someone with brains, certainly. Someone cunning and clever,' Inspector Kennedy affirmed. 'All this stuff about King Arthur, spooky dogs and the animal rights letters could be red herrings, to throw us off the scent, and the killing of this Asher woman might be another. Indeed, so might the fire-bombing of the activist.'

'The key to all this must be to work out how the killer got into and out of King's house in the first place,' Myres suggested with a wry grin, 'but the experts say it can't be done, so red herrings or not, they're all leads that have got to be followed up. I suppose that's what you want us and our teams for,' he went on, looking at Walsh directly.

'That's right,' Walsh said, rubbing his tired eyes. 'I'd like you, Kennedy, to tackle Asher. Find out her friends, acquaintances, and relations as well as relationships. If she knew something about her killer, and the killer knew that, then there must have been some communication between them. Question her neighbours about visitors and follow up the reports that are coming in about people seen in the Lammas Land and Sheep's Green areas. Myres, I'd like you to work on the

Ambrose fire-bombing. Delve into the Ambrose backgrounds – you never know, you might find some link with King or Asher – and organize a meticulous house-to-house questioning of the people on the estate where they live. Someone may have seen the bomber's car or means of transport. He couldn't have been on foot. The phone box used to send the warning was too far away for that. Ackers, you take over our files on the people who work at the laboratory. Interview them yourself, and find out what they were up to last night. Check them out thoroughly, particularly Dr Parkinson,' Walsh went on. 'So, if you three and your teams can handle all that, then we three can concentrate solely on the King killing.'

Walsh leaned back and looked at the row of faces again. 'Any questions? No? Good. Right then, I won't tie you down with special paperwork, you know what's needed and what's essential, but I will want a daily verbal report. So we'll all of us meet here, in my office, at eight thirty each morning, until the case is cracked. Best of luck.'

There was a period of silence when the other three had left. Reg took the opportunity to move to the chair directly opposite to Walsh's desk, where he could stretch out his long legs more comfortably. Brenda paced restlessly by the window. Walsh felt so tired it was difficult to make his brain work at all, but he knew he had to. If they were going to concentrate on King's killing, they must devise some strategic plan of action.

'A fat lot of use Forensic have been,' Reg remarked rather pointlessly.

'According to them the only way into that room without setting the alarm off is down the chimney, but that's only eight inches in diameter. Not a very likely route,' Brenda pointed out.

'We've got to be objective, boss,' Reg proposed, his fingers tapping spasmodically on Walsh's desk top. 'The only way into the room where King was killed is through the hall door –'

'Even though it was locked and bolted on the inside?' Walsh interrupted, fumbling in his pocket for his pipe and tobacco.

125

'Yes, Chief,' Brenda asserted positively. 'If the lock and bolt on that door were our only problem, we'd be all right. There's umpteen locked-room murder books been written – no doubt one of them has a solution that would fit our case. Strings and levers, I'd imagine.'

'Go on then, Brenda,' Walsh grunted. 'Now you've started, follow it all through.'

'OK, Chief,' she said brightly. 'Try this for size. Both the lock and the bolt don't fit in. The lock's the wrong sort and the bolt's unnecessary, so I propose that the killer, having dealt with King, changed the lock and fitted that bolt, as the first of the confusion factors.'

'We'd all got that far, Brenda,' Reg interposed dolefully. 'It just doesn't seem worth while taking it any further, not until we've found out how the killer got into and out of the house.'

'That's true, Reg, but that line of thinking presupposed that there would be an answer,' Walsh said thoughtfully, gently pressing down the tobacco shreds in the bowl of his pipe. 'Carry on with your theories, Brenda, but start at the beginning. The killer got in the house somehow, crept into the lounge . . .'

'. . . and caught the blissfully unsuspecting Arthur King unawares,' Brenda continued, 'having his bachelor-style supper in the chair by the fire. He was stunned by a blow to the head, using the Excalibur sword from the wall. Then King was laid on the floor, still unconscious, and Excalibur was driven into his chest; thereby setting us off on the Arthurian red herring.'

'You've missed a bit,' Reg smiled wryly. 'King's fingerprints were on both the lock and the bolt. Did the killer fit the bolt and change the lock before killing King? The body would have had to be dragged over to the door and back . . .'

'No, Reg. King would have been dead first,' Brenda went on, 'and his prints put on the lock and bolt before they were finally screwed on. Why go to all the effort and trouble of heaving an unconscious body across the room and back?'

'Yes, yes. No need to elaborate on that point, Brenda,' Walsh said impatiently. 'We'll accept that it was as you say. King was lying dead in front of the fire when his fingerprints were put on the lock and bolt. Go on with the strings and levers bit. How did the killer shoot the bolt, lock the door and remove the key, while he was standing outside the room?'

'Well,' Brenda started pensively, 'I don't suppose he used string as such, probably a strong nylon fishing line. Shooting the bolt would be easy. He'd line up the bolt knob with the slide, then double up a long length of line, put the middle loop over the knob, then run the doubled-up line down the room and round that window catch, the one which had the stay bar disturbed; then back under the door into the hall. All he had to do was pull both ends together to shoot the bolt, then draw on one of them to get his string back. He'd do something similar to turn the key too, only he'd need a short length of wood, something like a pencil, stuck in the hole in the handle of the key, to give the leverage for it to turn.'

'Fair enough, so far, Brenda,' Reg nodded, his shrewd eyes now showing more interest than they had earlier. 'But how did he get the key out of the lock? More levers and strings?'

'Possibly, but if it were me, I'd just tie a string to the key itself, and the lever, and run it round the back of King's easy chair and then under the door. That chair was nearly opposite. Pull the string and the key would come out of the lock, round the chair and under the door – the gap at the bottom is plenty wide enough, I think.'

'Nicely put,' Walsh said approvingly. 'But that presupposes that after the key was turned the flat head of the key lined up exactly with the slot in the lock. It wouldn't come out otherwise. Now, I wonder if that lock had been tampered with, to make the key line up. Packstone can tell us. I'll ask him.'

'Before you do, boss, there's one other point that might well be explained by all these strings going round the place,' Reg ventured, 'if Brenda's right and the strings were looped round the window stay bar pin. When the stay bar was dislodged the chances are the loop slipped off. If it then caught and twisted round the big Turk's head tassel knot on the end of the curtain puller, the killer would have had to tug pretty

127

hard to get his line free, and that could well have pulled the curtains open.'

'Yes, true, I don't think the killer expected that to happen,' Brenda mused. 'If those two bods who turned up later were expected to break in and generally mess up what little evidence there was in the house, it was because they could see King's dead body through that window that they scarpered.'

'Does it matter? Packstone and his experts say there's nothing wrong with the alarm system. While that's the case we're just wasting our time,' Reg said despondently.

'Don't be so damned negative, Reg,' Brenda snapped angrily. 'We won't get anywhere if you take that attitude.'

'I'm not being negative, I'm being realistic,' Reg retorted sharply. 'You may have explained a few minor problems. So what? You don't get any Brownie points for that.'

'Steady on, you two,' Walsh chipped in quickly. 'Trying to find out how the killer thinks, how his mind is working, is very important. We know that the killer came to King's house with a whole list of things to confuse us with, all of which must have taken him some time and trouble to prepare. Now, why?' Walsh relit his pipe and puffed out clouds of grey smoke. Reluctant though it might be, his brain was at least trying to work. 'Yes, I know they're to put us off the track, that's obvious, but surely it also means the killer thought that his tracks would be pretty obvious to us otherwise, and that if he didn't divert our attention in some way, he'd be in danger of being caught. Put it another way, if you'd made up your mind that you wanted to murder Dr King and at the same time knew that the chances of your getting on the suspect list were pretty slim, you'd just get on and do it, without pussy-footing about changing locks and bolts and things, wouldn't you?'

'You're merely thinking backwards and saying that the killer must be the most obvious, or one of the most obvious candidates, Chief,' Brenda stated, shrugging her slim shoulders impatiently. 'I'm not sure that helps us a great deal. What's obvious to the killer isn't necessarily what's obvious to us, and we don't know Arthur King's past like he probably does, so there may be many more names to go on the list.'

128

'Mrs King ought to be near the top of the list, boss, she's got two good motives. Revenge for being betrayed as a wife, and she gets all the family assets easily, rather than having to fight for a share in the divorce courts. She might have gone to Sainsbury's that night, but there was still time for her to go to the house and kill her husband,' Reg suggested.

'I favour King's sister, if what she said about her grandfather's will is correct,' Brenda stated. 'She now scoops all his fortune. She might try to give the impression that life's a bed of roses for her and her husband, but I'm not so sure that a pottery and art gallery set in the wilds of Norfolk could make a lot of money, or her husband's violins either, however good they are. Money might be more of a problem to her than she cares to admit. You ought to favour her too, Reg. She lives in Medraut House, and that's an alternative spelling of the Modred you've been looking for in your King Arthur business.'

'Those two are certainly possibilities,' Walsh agreed, 'but the one with the best opportunity is probably Parkinson, the director at the lab. Don't forget, he's got a similar sort of alarm installation in his own home, so he's got more chance than any of finding a chink in it, even if our experts can't find one. Obviously the pressure for King to replace Parkinson as boss was coming from the grandfather's shareholding. That may have eased because of the old man's senility, but those shares would probably become King's when his grandfather died, so Parkinson's problems hadn't gone away.'

'They're good motives, certainly,' Reg affirmed, 'but the one with the passion that could easily have turned into hate is Robin Redhead, King's old university chum. King pinched his Gwenda and married her. A fair while ago maybe, but time and brooding can turn resentment in a mind already sick into the kind of hatred that can kill, particularly if he still thinks he loves her and she him, or she would if King was out of the way.'

'There's others, even though the links aren't clear, Chief. I'm doubtful about that Dr Hammington, wandering about with a revolver. Maybe she did know King. It wouldn't be the first time a middle-aged woman fell for a younger man, and when rejected wanted revenge for being slighted. Then there's that Grant woman who was having the affair with King, and what about MacDunn, who installed the alarm system?'

'He's the least likely, Brenda. He only moved down from Edinburgh last year,' Reg pointed out. 'We can build up a list as long as our arm, but we've got to face up to it sometime. The experts say that nobody could have gone into and out of that house at that time.'

'Meaning,' Brenda interrupted scornfully, 'that it must have been suicide all along? Or was it done by Old Shuck, the phantom ghost dog? That explains everything, I suppose, the dog tracks as well. You may say that's logical reasoning, Reg, but I don't – besides, who killed Elizabeth Asher? Who fire-bombed the Ambrose house? Or are they just coincidences?'

Walsh looked down at his fingertips. This discussion was getting too heated, almost out of hand. Walsh glanced at Brenda's reddened angry face, then at Reg's long bony fingers which were tapping irritably on the far side of his desk, and for the first time for many years Walsh wished he could just get up and walk away from this job, leaving behind the responsibility, the stress, and the need to be an alert and objective leader of a specialist team. His team, if he didn't do something quickly, might just be starting to fall to pieces. Crime detection demanded a calm, resolute mind, but this bewildering impasse over the burglar alarm in King's house was preventing any of their projected sums from adding up. It was hard to accept that their only strategy was merely to follow up what might be red herrings in the blind hope that something would eventually make sense.

Walsh felt that he must find some inspiring words of encouragement that would bring back their confidence in their ability to solve any problem, however insoluble that problem might at this moment appear.

Such words did not come easily to a mind that was fighting its own depression.

He felt like a general of a hopelessly outnumbered army, surrounded and with nowhere to go but onwards into battle and certain death. What could be said to rally his dispirited troops – to enthuse them to continue the fight, even if it meant inevitable defeat? He had no idea what to say as he opened his mouth to speak. Of their own volition, out came the words: 'Into the valley of death rode –' but then there came a knock at the door.

'Come in,' Walsh shouted, thankful for the interruption.

Arthur Bryant came bursting in. 'The Volvo, sir,' he panted, having obviously run up the stairs and along the corridor. 'We think we've got a really good lead at last.'

'Thank the Lord for that,' Reg Finch said quietly, turning his head towards the newcomer.

'About time too, Arthur,' Brenda muttered mildly.

'Right, young Bryant,' Walsh said as calmly as he could. 'Put us in the picture.'

12

'Well, sir, Alison and me, we've been ringing round all the garages and breakers' yards again,' Detective Constable Arthur Bryant explained. 'I know we'd already asked them to tell us when someone came in for an old Volvo off-side front wing, but, well, you know what those kind of people are like. They say yes at the time, but the chances are it goes straight in one ear and out the other, or they have a day off and forget to tell anyone else about it. That's what happened in this case. The fellow we spoke to initially went off to stay with his sister in Brighton; never said a dicky bird to anyone else.'

'Get on with it, for Pete's sake, Arthur,' Brenda snapped impatiently. 'I've never known anyone rabbit on like you do.'

'That's not fair,' Arthur protested indignantly. 'You just complained that it'd taken too long to get results, and all I was doing was explaining the problems, so you'd understand why. You can't please some people.'

'It was very sensible of you to ring round the garages again, Arthur,' Reg murmured calmly, keeping back a hint of a smile, 'but which one came up with the goods in the end, and what were the goods?'

'Alison was in it as well as me, you know,' Arthur acknowledged generously. 'She's gone off to interrogate Vehicle-Records. She won't be long. We know the car number, you see. That's why we think this is such a good lead,' Arthur went on, ignoring the increasing signs of Brenda's impatience, but just then Alison Knott came in with a folded computer print-out, which she handed to Walsh.

'I found the owner, sir, on Vehicle Registrations,' Alison said calmly. 'And I checked to see if he was on Criminal Records too. He was.'

Walsh quickly scanned the sheets. 'The Dancer brothers? I don't know much about them. Anyway, finish your story, Arthur.'

'Yes, well, it was a breaker's yard near Chatteris, in the Fens. Yesterday a white Volvo with a crunched off-side front wing came in. As it happens they got all the bits they needed from an old black wreck, but the chap there made a note of the car number, the white Volvo, that is. He didn't ring and tell us, but there you go.'

'And one of the Dancer brothers owns the Volvo, I presume,' Walsh surmised.

Alison nodded. 'Yes. Ben Dancer, he's the older one. The other's Ern. They did a bit of house breaking when they were kids, but since then it's only been grievous bodily harm when they've had too many in the pub. Big men apparently, sullen and short-tempered – real Fen folk. They're contract plasterers by trade, and as you can see, they live in Tetling Fen, on the other side of Erith.'

'Right then, we'll go and see whether these two characters can shed some light on our darkness,' Walsh said. In spite of the signs of strain on his face he could still raise a smile at the prospect of taking positive action. If these two men, the Dancer brothers' had been one of Arthur King's murderer's red herrings, there must have been some verbal contact between them at some time. This could be the first direct link with the shadowy killer, and if they could get an accurate description from the two Dancer brothers, they might yet find a way to come home and dry on this murder case.

For the moment he felt quite optimistic, but then he hesitated. Two big men with short tempers and a record of GBH might just be a handful if things turned nasty, but if they all went, there would be five police officers. Only three of them males, certainly, but in a rough and tumble Brenda was worth a male and a half at least, and come to that, young Alison was no slouch either. The five of them should be sufficient.

'We'll take two cars,' he said finally. 'Alison, you can come with me as navigator.'

The Fens can have a strange effect on people. The vastness of a sandy desert or a wide snowy ice-field may make an individual seem appropriately small and insignificant, but the Fens can add a menacing, threatening feeling to that, which can send shivers down a sensitive spine.

Wide, open and exposed, usually under a low expanse of heavy cloud, the Fens are a black land of vast fields that stretch to infinity in all directions, with features dwarfed into insignificance. Mini Eiffel Tower pylons march slowly across the far skyline, telegraph poles are rows of tiny match-sticks which follow or cross the thin silver streaks that are water in the deep sharp-edged ditches and dikes, and the occasional stunted bush is in reality a full-grown tree.

That which was Tetling Fen huddled round a redundant grey steepled church, a two-pump garage and a one-roomed general store. The whole had an air of abandoned desertion.

Walsh drove slowly past a short row of bungalows and houses, staring at names and numbers, and found the very last building to be the one he wanted. It was a small, slate-roofed house with peeling paint and dingy net curtains; a rutted shingle drive led down the side to a miscellany of wooden and corrugated iron outbuildings. A rusty wheel-less van and a small trailer occupied much of the tussocky front lawn.

Walsh drew his car off the narrow road and on to the grass verge, as near as he dared to the edge of the inevitable ditch. There was no sign of life in the house at all.

'It rather looks as though no one's at home, boss,' Reg Finch ventured, shivering in the bitingly cold east wind, and turning back to his car for his thick quilted parka.

'I hope you're wrong, otherwise we're just wasting our time,' Walsh muttered. 'Come on, Alison, we'll try the front door. You three can go and see if there's anyone round the back.'

Brenda Phipps stepped delicately along the drive at first, trying to avoid the muddier patches and keep her boots clean, but it was obviously going to be a waste of time, so she gave that up and walked normally.

The area behind the house was more untidy even than that in front. Old fridges and car doors seemed the most popular items of rubbish to hoard. Brenda tried the back door, but that was locked, so she set out to explore the outbuildings. In the first, the largest, she found the old white Volvo, now with a black off-side front wing and bonnet.

'That looks as if it could be the one we're after,' Reg said, looking round the damp garage with its hard-packed earth floor. There was a bench along one wall with a vice, a few tools, a welder and more junk scattered about.

'The old wing's over there, in the corner,' Arthur pointed out. 'Forensic can do their paint tests on that if they have to.'

'Hopefully they won't need to, not if these two characters talk,' Brenda said. Then she heard the faint sound of tyres crunching gravel, and led the way outside.

The big Alsatian came round the side of the building at a run. It saw the three intruders and barked angrily while sinking back on its haunches. Then it bared its teeth in a low snarl and looked round as if undecided as to just what to do. It made up its mind, it charged.

Brenda gave a sharp cry of alarm, and stepped backwards hastily, while looking round for a way of escape.

She found herself being pushed roughly to one side by Reg

Finch. His watchful eyes were narrowed as he moved forward on his toes, appearing to brace himself in a futile attempt to withstand the full weight of the leaping animal.

However, at the very last moment, as nimbly as a boxer in the ring, Reg stepped sharply to one side, leaving his right arm invitingly outstretched. The hurtling dog's fangs sank into his quilted coat sleeve, just above the wrist. Then the dog was back to ground, scrabbling feverishly with his feet and growling furiously, pulling at the arm clenched between his teeth. But Reg had moved again, incredibly quickly. He had turned sharply as the dog had taken his arm so that now he was crouching astride the animal's broad back, gripping the writhing body between his legs. With his full weight pressing the dog into the muddy earth he grasped his right wrist with his left hand and started heaving the dog's neck backwards.

The dog was strong, and writhed and wriggled in an attempt to shake the man off, but Reg was gradually pulling its head further and further back, stretching and arching its neck until the bewildered growls became strangled gasps and the dog's lower jaw finally sagged open.

'Get a rope or something, for Christ's sake,' Reg snarled, his face contorted with the pain in his arm and the strain of the power struggle.

Brenda didn't move. What was happening before her eyes seemed to be as unreal as a slow motion movie, and she just couldn't get her limbs to move. But Arthur dived back into the garage. He'd seen some greasy rope in there, and a hammer. Maybe he could get the handle of that between the dog's teeth, then Reg could get his arm free. By the time he was back outside, however, the situation had again changed dramatically.

A big man had appeared at the corner of the building, and his face was reddening with anger.

'Let my dog go, you bastard,' he shouted, moving forward, obviously preparing for hostilities.

'Come any closer and I'll break its bloody neck,' Reg yelled in panic while craning his neck round, the better to see the newcomer.

'I can handle this one,' Brenda cried out, pulling herself out of her trance and moving forward to get more room to manoeuvre. That big dog may have caught her unawares but being faced by a single male, big though he was, held no fears for her.

How that confrontation might have ended up is speculation, because again the situation suddenly changed.

'Ben, you come away this instant,' screeched a little woman in a grey coat and black felt hat, who had now appeared on the scene accompanied by Walsh and Alison Knott. 'Don't you do nothing stupid now. You hear me! This here lot's police and I won't have no trouble.'

'Christ, mum, but look what he's doing to my dog,' the big man, Ben, protested. 'If he's harmed Jacko I'll kill him, so help me I will.'

'Jacko, you leave him. Right now, this minute,' Mrs Dancer screamed again. This time it was the dog who rolled his eyes at the sound of the woman's voice. 'Mister, you can let the dog go. He won't do no harm while we're here, honest.'

Reg looked doubtful, but gradually released the pressure on the dog's neck, found there was no more aggression, then drew his arm thankfully out of the jaws and got up.

'The one playing Tarzan is Detective Sergeant Finch, Mrs Dancer, and the others are Detective Constables Brenda Phipps and Arthur Bryant,' Walsh announced with a smile. 'As I say, we need to talk to your sons about an incident –'

'So you may, so you may,' the little woman said fearlessly, 'but you ain't in such a hurry as it can't wait till I takes me hat and coat off. Here, Ben, here's the stuff you wanted. You go and get that duck of yours cleaned up, that's the most important thing, then you can come along indoors and talk to this Inspector.' She handed Ben the plastic shopping bag. 'And you two constables can go with him if you think he might run away, but you, Mr Sergeant what's-your-name,' she looked directly at Reg, who was busy flexing the fingers of his right hand, 'you'd better let me have a look at that arm of yours. I don't reckon Jacko thought you was playing games. You can't blame him, though – you shouldn't go nosing round people's private property, even if you are police.'

Reg shrugged his shoulders and followed her into the house. There were many blue tooth-mark depressions on his arm, but none had breached the skin; nevertheless, the cold wet flannel held there was very soothing. It appeared that the thick parka jacket sleeve had prevented any serious injury.

Big Ben glared at Brenda and Arthur with undisguised hostility, and then strode over to the long low shed behind the garage.

'If you're coming in, shut the bloody door behind you,' he snarled.

Brenda looked about the dimly lit interior in surprise. It was heated by a small smelly paraffin stove standing by the door, but there were rows and rows of shelves along the wall containing cages, and those cages contained injured birds, and a few other small animals. In the one nearest to her was a falcon with a dingy bandage on its wing, another held a one-legged blackbird, and the next, a forlorn duck whose feathers glistened with oil.

Ben took a bottle of ordinary white spirit from the bag and picked up a rag, then reached in the cage for the oily duck. With surprisingly gentle hands he went to work, cleaning it up.

'You run a wildlife hospital, do you?' Arthur asked naïvely, pressing a fingernail against the bars of the blackbird's cage, causing the hopping inmate to hurry over to defend its territory with a flashing yellow beak.

'Well, it ain't a bleeding hotel, is it?' came the grunting reply.

The over-furnished little sitting-room was also overcrowded.

Once in there it was necessary to remain seated, for what space not taken up by a three-piece suite and a massive television was occupied by little china cabinets full of knick-knack souvenirs from seaside holidays.

'That was the night I spent over with my sister May,' Mrs

Dancer protested angrily, glaring at her two sons. 'You two promised me faithfully that you'd not get into any more trouble. I should have known better. Now, Ben, you're the oldest, you tell me the truth now, did you go down to this Badon Lane place like this here Inspector says?'

Big Ben swallowed hard, looked sheepish, then nodded reluctantly. 'Yes, mum, we did.'

'Did you take Jacko with you, and did he get out of the car?' Brenda asked.

'Did you?' Mrs Dancer repeated with another glare.

Again Ben nodded.

Brenda looked pleased. Obviously those dog prints outside Arthur King's house were those of Jacko the Alsatian. That finally put paid to Old Shuck, the phantom ghostly hound. All the weird happenings would have sensible explanations in due course, she thought confidently.

Walsh, however, was frowning. These were not the right circumstances for a questioning session in a murder inquiry. Mum, Mrs Dancer, was the dominant character in a situation in which he ought to be in control, even if she was quite clearly on his side in wanting to get at the truth. The fact that she sat in the armchair by the glowing electric fire, while he was crammed like a sardine in the middle of the settee, with Ern on one side and Brenda on the other, did not help, but it was necessary to bring some order into the questions, or else they'd be there all day.

'Let's start from the beginning,' he said loudly, with just enough aggression and authority in his voice to hold the others' attention. 'Just why did you both go to that house in Badon Lane? What were you after?'

Mum glared at Big Ben, but said nothing this time.

Ern screwed his face up as he concentrated hard. 'But, mum,' he said with an effort, 'we had to. That man there was wicked. He's killed lots of little dogs and rabbits and things, by sticking needles in them and making them go bad like.'

'That's right,' Ben confirmed, 'he'd give them diseases, and watch them suffer and die in pain. There's lots like him and the law don't stop them. That can't be right. All animals has got feelings, like you've said to us many times. We weren't going to do him no real harm, just rough him up a bit so he knew what a bit of pain was like himself. Maybe then he'd stop doing it.'

'I've said I don't agree with no violence, but I don't agree with downright cruelty either. Law or no law,' mum pronounced.

'How did you learn about this man and what he did?' Walsh wanted to know.

Both big men now seemed to have lost any fear or apprehension for their visitors.

'Fellah that brung things in told us,' Ern explained helpfully.

'Gerbil, he brought in first, then a cat, then that blackbird what's lost a leg,' Ben added.

'This fellow, was it his idea you should go and rough up the man who lived in Badon Lane?' Reg asked.

'Don't know about that,' Ben ventured with a puzzled look on his face, 'but I remember Ern saying we'd have to do it when mum weren't here, and us two were big enough to take anyone on.'

'And the next time he came he'd got that tree-lopping rope with the chain blade things in the middle. Said we'd have to cut the telephone wire if we were going to do the job properly. Well, we knew that, but I didn't think the thing would work, but it did.'

'And he said what was the best time to do it. Helpful, he was.'

'What was he like, this fellow? He didn't give a name and address by any chance, or any way you could contact him, did he?' Walsh asked hopefully, but both men shook their heads.

'He was only a little bloke. He weren't big enough to do the job himself,' Ern said helpfully.

'Wore them glasses with coloured lenses.'

'And a cap.'

'About her size, maybe,' Ben said, pointing at Brenda.

'A bit bigger'n her, but weedy like what she is.'

'He came in a car, presumably – did you see the number or the make?' Reg asked, for some reason finding it difficult not to grin.

'Red Metro.'

'Green Toyota.' Then both brothers shrugged their shoulders.

Jacko the dog wandered in and stood for a moment looking at the seated company, then padded over to push his muzzle between Reg's knees. His big brown eyes expressed a desire to be friendly with his one-time adversary. Reg scratched behind the big dog's ears, which was obviously just what was wanted.

'Did he speak with an accent? A Scottish one, perhaps?' Brenda asked.

'Not so's you'd notice. He was a bit gruff like, said he'd got a sore throat,' Ern explained.

'When you went out to this house in Badon Lane, you cut the telephone wires, what happened then?' Walsh inquired.

'We had a look in the front window and saw that bloke lying on the floor with a sword stuck in him. We didn't hang about, did we, Ben? Rare gave us the creeps,' Ern said, wriggling his shoulders to demonstrate the feeling.

'Then you hit another car as you drove away. Did you see anyone else hanging about?' Walsh asked.

'How did you know we hit a car?' Ern asked in astonishment.

'We didn't see nobody,' Ben answered.

'I don't think we've any more questions, at the moment. Thank you for the coffee, Mrs Dancer. It was very nice.' Walsh said, rising to his feet.

'You ain't going to charge my boys, are you? They didn't mean no harm,' Mrs Dancer asked anxiously as her visitors went out of the front door.

'I haven't made up my mind yet. Probably not, provided they keep out of mischief from now on,' Walsh replied glumly.

He'd desperately hoped to find a breakthrough in this Arthur King investigation; instead he'd found a couple of simple-minded toughs who'd obviously been set up to provide yet another red herring.

He told himself it was time to do some serious thinking, but that wasn't much help, he'd been trying to do just that for several days.

In the car going back, Brenda sat quietly for a time, lost in her own thoughts. When that Alsatian had come at her with its teeth bared, she'd felt scared stiff, and had only just stopped herself screaming out in sheer fright. She had to admit to herself that she just hadn't known what to do. She'd been on every sort of self-defence course going over the last few years, and had really thought she could hold her own anywhere. Yet now she knew there was a situation she couldn't cope with. If it hadn't been for Reg ... well ... Somehow he'd seemed to know just what to do, almost as though he'd done it before. Whether she'd have the sheer physical strength to pull a big dog's head back to the point where the neck might break was another matter – besides, deliberately letting a dog bite your forearm took a bit of nerve. It must have hurt like hell. Yet that was better than finding the dog's jaws at your throat.

'Reg, I'm sorry I snapped at you earlier on. My nerves are a bit on edge, I suppose,' she said quietly.

'Forget it,' Reg smiled. 'I probably deserved it. I was being a bit defeatist. It's a bit daunting, working on a case where you know that the forensic evidence will let any suspect we find off the hook.'

That wasn't the problem bothering Brenda just then though.

'Where did you learn how to tackle a big dog like that, Reg?' she went on.

'Oh, that,' Reg replied with a chuckle. 'I like dogs. I did a spell at the dog handlers' school years ago. I didn't stick it long because I always ended up as the chap the dogs had to chase in training; the man with the gun and padded arm. So I got used to the sight of them coming at me. I didn't always play things straight though. If you were quick, you could sometimes get them to take the inside of the padded arm, then you might be able to get them between your legs and sit on them. That's the safest place to be with a dog. You must stay on your feet whatever you do, you mustn't ever get knocked down. They learn quick, you don't usually catch them like that twice. Whether you could actually break a dog's neck as I conned

141

that fellow Ben I'd do, I don't really know. I wouldn't want to find out, frankly. I like dogs.'

Nothing was ever simple, Brenda thought. Obviously being quick and nimble was the key, plus the confidence in yourself that you could do it. Maybe if you were really quick getting behind the dog you could get your arms under its front legs and your hands round its neck in a double nelson, but it wasn't the sort of thing you could practise to find out, was it? The sight of that dog coming straight at her with bared teeth would form an ideal scenario for a nightmare, but, thankfully, she was never troubled by those – yet.

'You both did well to trace that Volvo,' Walsh said to the departing Alison and Arthur, in the Headquarters car-park. 'How do you fancy your chances of finding red Metros and green Toyotas with weedy drivers?'

'Mrs King's got a red Metro, boss,' Reg said, flexing his fingers and rubbing his arm again.

'And that woman who was having the affair with King, Anita Grant, she's got a green Toyota, Chief,' Brenda added.

Walsh sighed as he led the way to his office. 'I suppose I might have guessed that. This damned killer's still got us running round in circles. Reg, you ought to get that arm of yours X-rayed. I don't want you going off sick, not the way things are at the moment.'

'Maybe. I'll see what it's like in the morning,' Reg replied cheerfully.

'Please yourself. Well, we didn't learn much from that little trip, did we?'

Brenda looked surprised. 'Oh, I don't know, Chief,' she exclaimed. 'We now know where the dog prints came from, and it's quite obvious the killer expected the Dancer brothers to barge in on the scene of the crime, presumably hoping they'd make enough mess to cover any tracks he'd left.'

'And now we know what he looks like too, boss,' Reg said, grinning broadly. 'A weedy character, somewhat like our Brenda here.'

142

'Weedy? Me? I'll take you on any day of the week,' she challenged humorously.

Reg slipped his right hand in the front of his jacket. 'Oh yes, I suppose you would, now I've only got one good arm.'

Walsh smiled – at least his team was now in good spirits – and suddenly he felt more cheerful himself. 'I suppose if we can peel away all the red herrings like the skins of an onion, we might get somewhere eventually.'

'Sure we will, boss. It's as you said earlier, the killer probably thinks there's something about the way he did the murder that ought to be so obvious to us that the finger of suspicion would point straight to him. That's why he spread so many red herrings, and we now know the Dancer brothers were just another of those.'

'Yes, but that one didn't work out right because the curtains in that room were drawn back,' Walsh mused. 'Maybe your theory about the string round the window catch is right, Brenda. Obviously the killer didn't intend that. So two of his plans went wrong.'

'Three, Chief. Elizabeth Asher played some part in it, and she had to be killed to keep her quiet.'

'That's right, boss. Our killer probably isn't as cool and collected as we might think. He's not perfect, and I think he knows he's not, so it could be that he's mighty jumpy right now. Dreading the ringing of his door bell in case it's us after him.'

'Psychologically you could well be right . . .' Walsh agreed.

'If he's jumpy, maybe we could con him,' Brenda interrupted, her mind momentarily holding the picture of Reg sitting on the Alsatian's back, and with the big man Ben Dancer approaching. 'If we could con the killer into thinking we knew something, even if we don't, it might be that he'd panic and give himself away.'

'It's a thought, Brenda, but the key to all this is how the killer got through the burglar alarm system; if we knew that we'd probably have him, as we've said so many times before,' Walsh pointed out.

143

'But if the killer believed we were on the verge of finding that out . . .'

'I don't see how we could do that, Brenda. He must know that we've already had the whole system checked and checked again by experts,' Reg grunted.

Brenda was suddenly on her feet and pacing erratically about the room, her eyes gleaming with excitement.

'By George, I think she's got it, or I think she thinks she's got it,' Reg whispered, trying to sound like Rex Harrison in the *My Fair Lady* film.

'Chief, we need the experts' expert,' Brenda burst out. 'Who do the computer experts go to when they've got a problem they can't solve?' she demanded.

Walsh shrugged his shoulders. 'How the hell would I know?'

'Well, I know one of them. That chap Julian Fry, you know, the fellow I went to see to get a line on animal rights activists.'

'I remember, Brenda,' Reg smiled. 'You said he'd got a bad cold and didn't seem over-keen to co-operate with us.'

'So I did. Well, I'm sure he'd help us if his pal Professor Hughes asked him. That's right,' she went on, waving her hands about expressively. 'We'd need to go round all our suspects and drop out the fact that the experts' expert had agreed to look at King's system. If we say he's a genius who's never yet failed to solve a problem, the killer's bound to lose his cool. What else can he do, but try and bump poor old Fry off? But we'd be waiting, and,' she chopped her right hand expressively into the palm of her left, 'then we'll have him.'

'You know, boss, I think Eliza's got it, she's got it, she's got it,' Reg sang out cheerfully.

'Slow down, you two. Hold hard. Let's talk this thing through slowly, step by step,' but his own eyes were as bright with anticipation as theirs.

A well-planned ambush, catching the killer red-handed in the act of committing another murder, would be the ideal solution to their problems. Maybe the only solution.

144

13

Brenda Phipps felt that Professor Hughes's Downing College rooms were stuffy and over-warm, yet despite the overworked radiators and glowing fire the portly incumbent was attired in thick corduroy trousers and a roll-necked Fair Isle sweater of such vivid and vibrant colours as might be the envy of many a strutting bird of paradise. The heavy atmosphere was not improved by the Chief puffing on his pipe.

Having had the ambush plan outlined and explained to him, the professor was reacting with a disappointing lack of enthusiasm. He was just sitting in his chair, toying with his coffee cup and staring into the flames of the coal fire.

It was several moments before he spoke.

'I do see your problem,' he announced quietly. 'How ironic a situation it is for you both, to know that your technical and forensic specialists would be providing incontrovertible evidence that must acquit the guilty person, even if you could lay your hands on him.' He shook his head in evident sympathy. 'But I applaud the strategy of your thinking. Your killer has thwarted the use of logical reasoning, but I do agree with you, he might be under some psychological stress, and to increase that stress to breaking point might well flush him out of cover. Getting him to believe that you are on the brink of a solution to your alarm system problem could be one way of doing that.' Hughes leaned forward to put his cup on a nearby table.

'You might think I'm just rabbiting on a bit,' he went on, 'and so I am, but while I'm doing that I'm really pondering on the question of whether or not I should approach Julian with your proposition, as it stands, and I'm inclined to think that I should not.'

He looked at Brenda's disappointed face, and smiled. 'Oh, I've no doubt he'd agree to it, if I put it to him. He has much the same daring and yearning for adventure as I have, but it's far too easy to forget that the years have been passing us by. We may still have active brains, thank God, but our bodies no longer react to physical exertion as well as they once did. Not that we like to admit so, but I do fear that your proposition would put him in some danger. Your murderer sounds much too resourceful for my liking, and I would not want to have it on my conscience if my old friend's demise were to result from my intervention on your behalf.'

'You said, "as our proposition stands", Professor,' Walsh said quietly, undeterred by the other's long-winded verbosity. 'Do you have in mind any variations to it, that might make it acceptable?'

Edwin Hughes rubbed at his stubby nose and nodded. 'Yes, I do, as a matter of fact. I think if you were to substitute someone else to act as Julian, it might become acceptable. I can even suggest a suitable actor, or actress I should say.' He beamed cheerfully at his visitors. 'I do think that, with the application of some theatrical expertise, a grey-haired wig, perhaps, and some make-up, young Brenda here could be made to resemble Julian Fry sufficiently well for your purpose. She is about his height and although of course she is slimmer than he, there could be a little padding in the right places.'

'Excellent, Professor,' Walsh agreed, smiling broadly at Brenda's evident confusion at being cast so readily as the ideal player to act as an elderly man. 'You're quite right. We should have thought of that ourselves. Brenda will do it. It will be safer all round.'

'I think I'll invite Julian to spend a few days here with me while this is going on,' Hughes went on. 'There are some college events coming up that he might enjoy, then you can have a free run of his house in Ely. How soon can you set up your ambush, Inspector? Assuming, of course, that he agrees to the proposal.'

'Twenty-four hours. No, best say thirty-six hours, Professor,' Walsh estimated.

'Let's say tomorrow night then. Right, I'd better stir my stumps and get over to see him. These things are best done face to face, rather than by telephone, don't you think?' Hughes said cheerfully. 'It's all very exciting. I'll be in touch.'

'I don't know where you get your crazy ideas from, Sidney, really I don't,' the CC said, shaking his head scornfully. 'You're really scraping the barrel with this one. No, you're not! You're like a drowning man, clutching at straws.'

'What the hell else can we do?' Walsh responded sharply. 'We can't dispute the pathologist's report – we wouldn't want to anyway, because he's right and King was murdered. We can't dispute Packstone's experts either. So, if we want to solve this case, somehow or other we've got to get the killer to betray himself, and I can't see a better way than this, can you?'

'Just because you're going round and round in bloody circles, you think you can hit your target by flipping off orbit at a tangent. How you've conned old Hughes and this Fry into your kooky scheme I do not know,' the CC growled.

'That was no problem. Fry took a fancy to young Brenda when he realized that she knew pretty well as much about his precious porcelain figurines as he did.'

The CC jerked his head disdainfully. 'There's no fool like an old fool, and I reckon you'll be joining him on the nut farm soon, Sidney. Just supposing the killer is on your short list and you are able to drop out the fact that this marvellous computer expert Julian Lancelot Fry is going to solve your murder mystery; even the most simple-minded berk will spot that it's a trap. Besides, who the hell has ever heard of this Julian Fry? Let alone know that he lives in Ely? You're nuts, Sidney. If you put the wind up this killer, all he'll do is a bunk to Argentina, or Chile, or some such place. Then we'll spend the next five years, and God knows how much of our budget, trying to get him extradited.'

If the CC thought this tirade would demoralize his Chief Inspector of Serious Crime, he was mistaken.

Walsh's tired face creased into a good impression of a Cheshire cat's grin, and he passed a sheet of paper over the desk. 'He'll know all about Fry if he reads the local paper. That's going in tonight's edition; middle-page spread.'

The CC found himself looking at a rather fuzzy photograph, and then he read a draft of a newspaper article expounding the fact that Fry was the world-famous, Ely-based computer genius who was, metaphorically, about to rub salt in the wounds of all the other top experts – by tracing the whereabouts of the missing pension fund millions, thereby earning himself the undying love, affection and adulation of millions of hard-done-by old-age pensioners, and also a King Arthur or Robin Hood-sized place in the folkore of the future.

The writer of the article had waxed eloquent – with a vengeance.

The CC's jaw dropped, momentarily. 'Who the hell wrote all this tripe?' he spluttered.

'Fry himself,' Walsh replied smugly. 'Apparently he's got a book half written, in the style of a detective story, about all the computer-based fraud crimes he's solved. He reckons the advance publicity could help to make it a bestseller. The deal with the newspaper is merely that we give their reporter a head start when we've cracked the murder case.'

The CC shook his head and his expression was deadly serious. 'This killer is about the cleverest and coolest of characters that you've ever come up against, Sidney. If you're not on the ball, all that might come out of it is this old fellow Fry getting a premature entry into a six-foot-deep hole. Then we'll all have a load of egg on our faces.' From the inflexions in his voice, the latter appeared the more heinous crime.

Walsh shook his head 'If it goes wrong it won't be old Fry who gets hurt, it'll be young Brenda Phipps. She's doing the stand-in part.'

The CC waved a hand in the air. 'Spare me any more details. I don't want to know. I won't get any sleep as it is, worrying about what you and your cowboys are getting up to. Be it on your own head, but you let me know what happens, pronto. Right?'

Inspector Kennedy was the first to arrive in Walsh's office.

He sat himself down in the chair favoured by Reg Finch, the one directly opposite Walsh's desk. 'We should have interviewed all the owners of the cars parked near where Asher was killed by tonight,' he announced. 'I'll go through them first, and see what leads there are, if any. Her neighbours have given us some descriptions of people who've visited her, but they're vague, as you'd expect. The photofit team'll be working on them this afternoon, so we might get something there,' he went on, flipping through the pages of his notebook. 'You know she'd been married twice? She was only eighteen, first time. That didn't last long – about a year. That bloke married again, he lives local, got three kids now. The second time for her lasted a bit longer, about three years. A nice chap, works for the university. I saw him myself. Seems whatever he did for her was always wrong, but even then she moaned that he was putting it on her. Poor chap reckoned that when she walked out on him it was the happiest day of his life. There's also a couple of aunts and cousins to see, yet.'

Then Detective Constable Ackers arrived. 'Morning, sir,' he said to Walsh and nodded to Kennedy. 'I've done preliminary interviews with all the lab staff. I'll go through what I've got this evening, and work out a strategy for my next move. Mostly I've concentrated on the Elizabeth Asher angle, you'd mostly covered the King side. I thought that'd help The Fiddler, here,' he went on, jerking his head in Kennedy's direction and receiving a scowl in return. Obviously Kennedy was not enraptured by a nickname that referred to his violin-playing namesake. 'Most of the files you'd already started, Inspector, were on the more senior staff. I'm not saying that's not right, of course, for there's some right weird characters among them. Enough complexes to keep a head-shrinker in business for years, particularly Parkinson and Peters. A right couple of nuts they are, and there's a lot of in-fighting been going on lately that I haven't unravelled yet. It seems you were right about King's attempt to get rid of Parkinson. It didn't come to anything, but Parkinson was dead worried, so the others say, but they're all like a load of kids, back-biting and making snide remarks. The problem's going to be sorting out the wheat from the chaff. I haven't linked Parkinson with Asher in any way yet, but that Grant woman, the one who was having the affair with King, you should hear some of the things she says about him. You'd think she wouldn't have touched him with a barge pole, let alone slept with him. Bailey's the only one I've really sussed out. He's a keep-fit nutter, an overgrown schoolboy. Everything's got to be done in double quick time, better and faster than anyone else, except sitting down and thinking things out first. He'd have made a good officer in the First World War trenches. A real "come on" man – he'd have got all his troops wiped out in double quick time.'

'There's a lot like him about,' Detective Sergeant Myres interrupted as he shut the door behind him. 'Sorry I'm a bit late, Inspector. Traffic,' he explained. 'Finch and Phipps'll be up in a minute. They drove in as I came up the stairs. I haven't a lot to report. We've still got to finish the house-to-house questioning of those people who weren't at home yesterday. There's two or three reports of a noisy car going off at speed, shortly before the fire engines rolled up. Rough silencer, throaty roar, a bit like a Formula One, are all the descriptions we've got, but we've a lot more to do, yet.'

'Excellent. Right, now we're all here,' Walsh said, as the final pair arrived. 'Thanks for the briefings. There's another purpose to this meeting,' and he outlined the scheme to lure Arthur King's killer into an ambush.

Two of the faces of those hearing the plan for the first time remained resolutely impassive, while the third, that of Myres, if anything looked more gloomy. 'It's a bit of a long shot, but I've heard worse,' he muttered, indicating to those who knew him that he'd given a guarded approval. Some years earlier Myres had inherited an old trunk full of ancestral papers and letters, and had discovered that he had a relative who'd taken part in Wellington's Peninsular assault on the fortress of Badajoz. That relative had been a member of the unsupported 'Forlorn Hope' team's attempt to scale the unbreached walls, far away from the main attack. Sustained courage and determination had made that attempt a successful one. Myres had been so affected by the tale that he had vowed to friends that he would find out about more such Forlorn Hope ventures in battle, and immortalize them all in a book. Unfortunately an inordinate amount of time and travel was needed to research such information, and so his project had progressed slowly; so slowly that his friends were apt to say, somewhat unkindly, that his venture itself was likely to form at least one chapter in his book, if not the bulk of it.

'I see,' Inspector Kennedy said thoughtfully. 'When Fry comes back from London on the train this evening, Brenda switches for him in the men's loos while he changes trains on Cambridge station; and she goes on to Ely instead. Today's Friday, so the killer's got the whole weekend in which to work. That means at least forty-eight hours of intensive surveillance. It'll take all of us, and more, to provide that sort of cover, especially if you also want a tail on each of the prime list suspects.'

'That's right,' Walsh agreed, 'and I do. If it's not done properly, there's no point in doing it at all.'

Ackers nodded his agreement. 'But it'll mean putting our investigations on ice for a while, though.'

'Inevitably,' the Forlorn Hope expert admitted, 'but it also means we've got to think up some good reasons for re-interviewing those people on the list.'

'And', Brenda interrupted, 'working out some way of dropping Dr Julian Fry's name as the expert, without making it too obvious.'

'Is this Fry really going to do his stuff on King's alarm system?' Kennedy asked.

'I shall pick up a new duplicate alarm control system and copy program from MacDunn, he's the man who installed the system in the first place,' Walsh explained, 'and take them to Fry's house early in the evening, just as anyone watching would expect, but it'll be Brenda there, not Fry, won't it? Now, we've a lot to do. First we'll go through the prime suspect list, then we'll tackle a surveillance roster, starting with a minder on Liverpool Street station keeping an eye on Fry till he gets to Downing College where he's staying for the weekend. Young Arthur Bryant can handle that, I think.'

Walsh rang the bell of MacDunn's flat, but the door wasn't opened by the alarm installer. Instead, he found himself gazing into a pair of strangely familiar big blue eyes that twinkled with amusement at his momentary surprise.

'Come in, Inspector,' the young woman said with a friendly smile, opening the door wide. 'Jim's been called out, but he said you'd be coming, and asked me to stay until you arrived. I didn't mind,' she explained. 'I wasn't doing anything important.'

'I remember now,' Walsh said, having racked his brains to recall the girl's name. 'You're Jean – the puppet-maker.'

'Now, how did you learn that?' she replied, opening the blue eyes even further. 'It doesn't matter. You'd expect a Detective Chief Inspector to know everything, wouldn't you? I'm just making coffee, would you like one? It's no trouble.'

Walsh nodded. 'Yes, please. White with two.'

The girl was a little on the stout side, and her face, though pretty, seemed plainer than he'd remembered it from the other evening, but viewing those wondrously fine eyes was a treat in itself, particularly if you felt you were immune to their effects.

A few moments' chat while he drank the coffee should give him ample time to mention Julian Fry's name. He would just have to hope that this Jean relayed the information to MacDunn later. It was a confounded nuisance – now he'd be worried that perhaps one person on his prime suspect list

152

mightn't be aware of the vital piece of information which was the bait for the trap. All ambush schemes relied to a certain extent on luck, this one probably more than most.

However, he needn't have worried, for Jean herself gave him the ideal opportunity to pass the information on.

'Jim said he needed to know who was actually having this control box,' she explained after she'd brought the coffee cups into the sitting-room. 'He says he's got to book it out to someone, otherwise he'll get accused of pinching or losing it.'

Walsh shrugged as he reached to take the cup she offered him. 'He'll get it back unharmed, but he can either book it to me or Dr Julian Fry. It doesn't matter which. Puppet-making's your hobby, is it?'

'Not really, just something to do when there's nothing on the telly. Fry? That name sounds familiar,' Jean said rubbing her chin thoughtfully.

Walsh shrugged again. 'He had his face spread all over the middle page of the local rag yesterday,' he said casually. 'What do you do for a living?'

'Me? I teach at the polytechnic – business studies,' she replied, turning the brightness in her eyes up a watt or two.

Walsh grinned. 'I should imagine puppet-making is a good way of relaxing after trying to drum double-entry bookkeeping into people's heads all day.'

That builder fellow would be the next person to see. That would need a phone call first, because the chances were that the man would be out on site somewhere. He also needed to pop into the office before he went out to Fry's house in Ely. There were plenty of reports and files that he could take with him to read over the weekend, while he was waiting for the trap to be sprung. He wouldn't be talking to Gwen tonight either. He'd explained about the ambush plan when she'd last rung. He'd be incommunicado for a few days. It was funny how a hard, tough nut like him could miss someone as much as he was missing Gwen. It was even stranger to actually hear himself telling her just that. Normally the best way of keeping one's emotions under control was to button up and say nothing at all. Still, she'd be home next Thursday.

In the mean time, there was much to be done.

He looked at his watch and finished his coffee. 'That was lovely, thanks,' he said to the girl with the beautiful blue eyes.

Now he'd better collect his parcels, and get on.

'Good afternoon, Mrs King,' Reg Finch said cheerfully. 'May I come in for a few moments? We're rather keen to have that anonymous letter you were sent, if you've managed to find it,' he went on. That was a good enough reason to get him in the house, and she was bound to ask him how the investigation was proceeding, then he could rabbit on a bit about the Forensic department being very busy, before dropping out Julian Fry's name and saying it all ought to be wrapped up pretty quickly when the experts' expert had done his stuff.

Then there was the Arthurian Society. Fortunately the Reverend was obviously such a gossip that the snippet about Julian Fry being about to solve the problem of King's murder was bound to be spread far and wide in no time at all.

After that he needed to pick up some changes of clothing before going out to the house in Ely.

It was all going to work out reasonably well. Margaret, his social worker wife, was going to take advantage of the ambush plan, which would have left her on her own, by spending a long weekend with her mother in Yorkshire. He, with Alison Knott and the boss, would be the inside team, minding Julian Fry, alias Brenda Phipps. The boss had glared a bit in disbelief when Reg had declared that he was fully fit and that his right forearm was giving no trouble, even though it still ached at times. If there was going to be any action, then it would be in the Ely house, and, arm or no arm, that's where Reg wanted to be.

'Did Elizabeth Asher get on well enough with King for them to have exchanged confidences, do you think?' Detective Constable Ackers asked of Anita Grant.

'I wouldn't have thought so,' she replied, raising her eye-brows disparagingly, 'but it depends on what you mean by confidences. He'd get her, we all did, to do the odd bit of shopping for us, especially if she had to pop into town on business. What did you have in mind?'

'I was thinking of King's security alarm code.'

'No chance. Arthur wasn't that daft.'

'Was Asher bright enough to be able to understand com-puter programs, how they work, I mean? Could she have made changes to King's alarm system program, if she'd got her hands on it?'

Anita Grant shook her head. 'No way. She had more than enough trouble working her word processor.'

Ackers looked disappointedly down at his notebook. 'Oh well, never mind,' he muttered in a low voice. 'The very best guy in the land's going to be sorting King's alarm pro-gram out.'

'You mean you've got Julian Fry helping you?' Anita said in some surprise. 'Lord, someone must have pulled some strings then. He doesn't come cheap either, but no doubt the poor old taxpayer will dig in his pocket, yet again.'

'You know this man Fry then?' Ackers said apprehensively. It had occurred to none of them that there might be even the remotest possibility that someone on their suspect list might know Fry personally.

'Only by reputation, more's the pity,' Anita Grant admitted with something akin to a smirk. 'He was still being talked about by the tutors in my old college when I was there. He was the heart-throb of their student days. Loved by all, they say, except husbands and boy-friends, of course.'

Dr Julian Lancelot Fry pushed tentatively at the door of the far end cubicle in the men's loo on Cambridge railway station, and stepped inside. The shock of suddenly coming up against one's own mirror image anywhere, let alone in that unlikely setting, was almost certain to engender some sort of verbal reaction, but when Fry opened his mouth to conform, his image put a slender finger to its lips, to warn of the necessity for silence, then reached forward to undo the buttons on his light-coloured suede coat. He turned in the confined space so that it could be more easily slipped from his shoulders, then wriggled into the strange dark blue trench coat that was handed him. His hat was changed for a cap, tinted spectacles were pushed on his nose, then, most difficult of all, his brown shoes were changed for black.

His image was ready before he was; it picked up the black document case, closed one eye in a conspiratorial wink, then pushed past him out of the door.

Fry slid the bolt quietly closed to ensure that he was not interrupted, and tied his shoes properly while waiting the stipulated five minutes before re-entering the outside world. He then proceeded to walk the half-mile or so to Downing College.

He felt uneasy in his unfamiliar clothes, as though in some way part of his personality had been taken from him, and certainly age had deadened his once normal reactions to the close proximity of an attractive woman, but he entered into the spirit of acting the part of someone other than himself by hunching his shoulders and trying to walk with a heavy, flat-footed tread, instead of his normal jaunty stride.

14

'My feet are killing me,' Brenda Phipps said emphatically, kicking off Julian Fry's shoes without bothering to unlace them, and sitting down in one of his sitting-room chairs. 'I didn't realize it was quite so far from the railway station.'

'I must say, you really do look the part,' Alison Knott said admiringly.

'You've missed your true vocation, Brenda,' Reg added with a smile. 'Mrs Phipps's little daughter should have gone on the stage.'

Brenda scowled back. 'Yes, I know, the one that's leaving

in twenty minutes. It's all right for you two, all you've got to do is sit around polishing your backsides for a couple of days, while I do all the hard work. I hope that one of these days we'll have to do an ambush with you dressed up as a long skinny woman, Reg, then maybe you'll have a bit more sympathy.'

'Not my style, love, dressing up as women,' Reg smirked smugly. 'Whereas the part you're playing seems made for you. You make a superb old man, but you really must learn to accept the applause of your audience with a little more decorum. No, don't take that wig off. Lord, you'll ruin everything.'

'Don't panic, Reg,' Brenda replied calmly, scratching at her head vigorously. 'It gets so hot in that thing, it makes me itch,' but she slipped it back on, and patted the replica of Fry's silvery-white locks into order. 'It's a nice place our friend Julian Lancelot's got here,' she went on, but neither of the others seemed interested in a general conversation. Already mentally prepared for a long near-silent vigil, they had plenty of books and papers to occupy their minds.

So Brenda sat back in the chair and looked about the room again. Fry's porcelain collection was still tastefully displayed, and inspecting that, piece by piece, was going to be one of her main occupations this weekend.

Ambushing with the Cambridgeshire Constabulary had obviously moved up a gear into the luxury-venture class. In recent years she'd hidden behind trees and wardrobes or lain in wait under damp shrubs. Then she'd needed dark clothes with black greasepaint smeared on her face and hands, but this time the greasepaint was variously coloured and artistically applied to create the lines and wrinkles of an elderly man. Neither was there a need to cower out of sight in frozen immobility; she had to move about to mimic Julian Fry's weekend life-style, and merely wait for someone to try and kill her. Her heart beat a little faster at that thought. In what form would the attempt come? If indeed it were to come at all. It was unlikely to be an open frontal attack; she would prefer that, given a choice in the matter. If the killer could somehow work his way in

157

close, it would probably be a quick knife thrust in the ribs, if not, maybe the deed would be done by a torso-aimed bullet, fired from a distance. The long, lightweight flak jacket under her shirt, which also helped to thicken her slender feminine form into that of a man, would prevent either of those being fatal. Painful perhaps, but not deadly. Otherwise she had to be prepared for a skull-crushing blow, or the garrotting that the killer had already used successfully on Elizabeth Asher. The alternatives would be smothering with a pillow or poison in her food. The latter would not work, though; they would only be eating the meals they'd brought with them. As to the rest of the options, well, she'd have enough 'minders' to guard her, particularly when the Chief arrived; and they were all trained experienced professionals, just as she was herself. See Reg there, pricking up his ears as that car went past, even though he was apparently engrossed in the King Arthur book by Geoffrey Ashe. No, she was safe enough, provided they all, herself included, maintained their high standards of vigilance.

That thought made her wriggle her toes guiltily. She got up to go and find an extra pair of socks that would stop her feet slipping about inside Fry's shoes. After that she'd make some coffee and reread the notes Fry had made on his usual weekend routines. It was never wise to take chances, because she'd only got one life, and it was a good one. Sometimes she got a bit lonely on her own, but one thing was for sure, she wasn't going to lack good company this weekend.

Three of the constabulary's 'old van' surveillance vehicles were already parked in carefully chosen positions from which their hidden occupants could observe the approaches to Julian Fry's house. A fourth would be used later, so that the others could be relieved in turn. Fortunately the house was in a wide cul-de-sac, over which the looming bulk of the nearby cathedral seemed to throw a protective cloak of peaceful tranquillity. Access on foot, however, was not so easy to control. There were a number of back paths and narrow lanes linking the cul-de-sac to adjacent roads, and so the other two vans kept watch where those allowed an approach to the rear of the house.

Walsh's arrival with the duplicate of Arthur King's alarm control box was an apparently innocuous event, yet it had been planned with some care. It was considered necessary for Walsh, or someone like him, to be seen to drive away. So, after a few minutes, when the occupant of the surveillance van considered that there was no one to observe the fact, Arthur Bryant wriggled from the back into the car's front seat, and drove away.

Now, as far as the perpetrators of the ambush were concerned, the trap was set.

'It's unlikely that anyone'll try coming in from the front, boss,' Reg said. 'The street lighting's fairly good.'

Walsh nodded. 'The back of the house is the most vulnerable. I wouldn't say our two rear vans are completely useless, but any enterprising person could slip over a few garden walls into this place and use a crow bar on the back door. Nevertheless, we'll stick to our original plan. At night Alison will be in the main bedroom's bathroom annexe. I'll be in the small bedroom opposite, and you, Reg, base yourself in the corner of the sitting-room where you can see through the doorway into the hall and the bottom of the stairs. During the day one of us will be in the rear utility room, to cover the kitchen and the back door, another in the cupboard under the stairs, to be on hand for a front-door caller, and the other one can rest and get some sleep. Any questions? Right, we'll go on silent routine from now on. Don't forget that Brenda's supposed to be the only one in the house, so keep away from the windows. Only she may put lights on and off when she moves about, and, particularly important, only she may flush the toilet or pull the plug out of the wash-basin. It's basic stuff, I know, but it's easy to forget.'

* * *

The night passed peacefully into a morning of watery sunshine, with no incidents.

Brenda had surprised herself. With Julian Fry's warm colourful pyjamas over her flak jacket, she had actually dozed off in his comfortable bed. Since she was unsure whether she should be proud of this as a demonstration of her imperturbability under stress, or ashamed of it as a lack of vigilance, she made no mention of the fact to the others.

The milkman delivered, closely followed by the paper-boy. Later the postman pushed some letters and a small narrow parcel through the letter box, but there was no need to fear that it contained a bomb. The radio had pre-warned of its arrival, and confirmed that it had been checked at the sorting office. Mid-morning, a jaunty dapper Julian Fry look-alike set off for a short stroll, preceded at a distance by a rather scruffy Ackers, and followed by an equally scruffy Bryant.

The sun struggled for a while against the low hazy clouds, but by late afternoon it had given in to a misty drizzle.

In the early evening Brenda put the television on for the news, and drew the curtains on the darkening world outside.

Later, as she was crossing the hallway to the kitchen to make herself a coffee, there came a short, unheralded ring of the front door bell.

She clipped the chain into place before cautiously opening the door a few inches.

Then she found herself reeling backwards in confusion, as the door was burst wide open, wrenching the securing chain's puny one-inch screws clean out of the woodwork.

Two burly figures rushed in. The first wielded a short heavy hammer in a raised right hand that was already swinging viciously down. To avoid the blow Brenda had to jerk herself to one side, but since she was already tottering backwards, that made her lose her balance completely and caused the wig of silvery-grey hair to slip forward over her face, masking one eye. As she fell she made a spirited response by kicking at her assailant's groin with both feet, but she missed, giving him only a glancing blow on the thigh. A heavy boot kicked at her ribs and sent a sharp rasping pain through her chest in spite of the cumbersome flak jacket. Now on the floor, she tried to wriggle away by scrabbling on the carpet with heels and elbows, but her shoulder was up against the skirting board and she could get no purchase. Through her one clear eye she saw that hammer start on another downward journey, straight for her head. Her squirming would not get her clear this time, and the arm she was raising as a shield was only a puny defence. That heavy metal head would crunch and smash through bone and tissue with consummate ease. Even if she still lived after that blow had landed, she would probably be permanently maimed and her face disfigured, and very likely she would be blind as well, never again to see the glowingly rich colours of a Meissen piece or a Coalport figure. All this was only a fleeting vision of an impending hell on earth. She opened her mouth to scream in terror, but no sounds came.

Suddenly another arm came into sight, a strangely long black arm, that swept the falling hammer head harmlessly to one side. Then, as if in slow motion, a second black arm appeared near her face, this one with a huge clenched fist on the end of it. Like a rocket it swept upwards, to explode with a resounding crack on her assailant's jaw. The accompanying cry of pain, however, seemed to come from the deliverer, because the receiver just crumpled soundlessly backwards, and fell with a thud to the floor.

Her assailant's accomplice was faring only marginally better. He had suffered from a surprise flank attack as Walsh had come charging out of the sitting-room like a rampant bull. Now that accomplice was helpless in a full nelson and in imminent danger of having his head used to demolish a number of Julian Fry's beautifully turned oak stair rails.

That honour was denied him by the appearance of a steely-eyed Alison Knott from upstairs, come hot-foot to join the fray, prepared to use the pair of handcuffs she clasped in her gloved right hand as a highly reprehensible but efficient knuckle-duster.

She appeared to be somewhat regretful as she used them conventionally to secure the hands of the still-conscious intruder behind his back.

161

'Are you all right, love?' Walsh said gruffly to Brenda. He was breathing so hard that the words formed stiffly and jerkily.

'I reckon so,' Brenda replied, allowing Reg Finch to pull her to her feet with his left hand. Nevertheless, she presented a strangely ghoul-like appearance, with her dishevelled wig and smeared greasepaint.

Walsh seemed satisfied, though. The trap for the killer of Arthur King and Elizabeth Asher had been cunningly set, and it had been sprung, if under somewhat unexpected circumstances. There had been long odds against it, but it had happened, and now he could reap the triumphant rewards by identifying Arthur King's killer.

'Who have we got here, then?' he said ecstatically, turning the handcuffed man so that he could see his face; but the face was that of a stranger.

He was stubbly-cheeked with a gold ring in one year, a scar under the left eye, and the hair on his head barely an inch long all over. A male, five foot tennish, twelve and a half stone, in his early twenties.

'Who the hell are you?' Walsh growled in intense disappointment. 'Let's have a look at the other one.'

The other, too, was a stranger. A male . . . stubbly-cheeked . . .

Walsh looked gloomy and tried to force his brain into action.

The worst of all possible scenarios appeared to have unfolded before his eyes. He really could not bring himself to believe that these two characters were directly involved in King's and Asher's murders, yet neither could he convince himself that their appearance here was only by coincidence. It rather looked as though the killer had used these two hoodlums to either spring the trap or permanently put Dr Julian Fry's computer-logic brain out of action.

There had always been a possibility that the killer would not act in person, but when you set up an ambush you could not dictate your own terms. They'd stirred King's killer into action certainly, but he had outwitted them. There remained just one more chance of success, if the killer was still in the vicinity, watching.

'Surveillance teams! Grab hold of anyone you can see,' Walsh snapped out desperately into his radio telephone.

Now there was something else for him to worry about, judging by the concern the others of his team were showing for the unconscious man on the floor.

'I think this one needs medical attention, sir,' Alison Knott announced abruptly, bending to raise one of the prone man's eyelids, then to feel at the base of his neck. 'He's got a pulse, but it's a bit slow. I think I've seen his mug before. Petty break-ins, GBH, or something like that, but he'll be on our records.'

People injured by police activity, however guilty of violence themselves, could cause a whole heap of trouble if allegations of excessive use of force were made to the Police Complaints Board.

'Get a doctor and an ambulance,' Walsh growled, trying to fight against a resurgent feeling of depression.

'You caught him a hell of a whopper, Reg,' Brenda said, starting to wipe the greasepaint from round her eyes with a handkerchief, having already removed the wig. 'I heard something crack when you hit him. You'd better let me have a look at your hand.'

Reg Finch winced as she touched it.

'You've either bust that middle finger or dislocated it,' she diagnosed, trying to sound calm and complacent lest her voice betray other emotions. That was twice in as many days that Reg had come to her rescue. The trap had been sprung so quickly by the bursting open of the front door that she'd been off balance and on the defensive right from the start, and once again she'd played no real part in the action.

'What the hell were you two playing at, letting these characters get right up to the front door without warning us?' Walsh snarled angrily at one of the watchers from the surveillance van at the end of the road.

The watcher shrugged his shoulders and scratched his head. 'I dunno for sure, sir. It's so misty out there that you can't see properly without keeping the wipers on the van going, and we couldn't do that,' he said, clearly highly embarrassed. 'There was a whole group of lads went down the road a while ago, and out through that passage at the far end, on the right. Larking about they were. These two must have slipped in the gate as they went past, while the others covered them. Sorry, but –'

'You can go with this bod to the hospital. See if you can do that without losing him,' Walsh snapped. 'Reg, you go too, and get that hand of yours fixed up. Right, let's hear what our handcuffed charlie here's got to tell us. Bring him in the kitchen.'

But once seated at the oak table Walsh didn't start asking questions straight away. Interviewing techniques needed to be varied to suit the circumstances. Instinctively Walsh felt that to begin barking out questions would only increase the surly individual's obvious stubbornness. So he set out to tell a story that might well bring some co-operation.

'You two were set up, you know,' he said. 'As sure as eggs is eggs. A right couple of fat pigeons you and your mate are. Shall I tell you what you don't know? Someone is gunning for the fellow that lives here. There's a big fat contract out for whoever does him in. Whoever set you up knew we'd probably be hanging around, and he wasn't going to risk his pretty little neck. Not likely! Not when there's mugs like you about.' So far so good, Walsh thought. After the 'big fat contract' bit, the chap was clearly listening, and looking thoughtful.

'What were you told? That there was loads of cash in the house, or were you offered a couple of hundred to get the man's briefcase? It doesn't matter! What he wanted you to do was beat the chap here up good. Yes, and take the rap – for murder. That's right! If we hadn't clobbered you, he'd have come in, when you'd gone, to finish the old man off good and proper. Then he'd have scarpered, leaving your marks all over the place, and he'd probably have tipped us off about you too, just in case we were too thick to pick you up on our own. Then he'd have been off to the Bahamas with thousands of pounds tucked in his money belt, laughing all the way, and where would you two be going, having done his dirty work for him? Into clink for life, that's where.' Walsh paused to feel for his pipe and tobacco. He hadn't smoked it for over twenty-four hours now, because Fry wasn't a smoker, and such smells in his house would have been a dead give-away. Now he needed one to soothe his nerves.

'You know,' he went on, 'I'm not really interested in you, or your mate. The chap I'm after is the fellow who set you up. If you help me get him, maybe I'd help you. Maybe I could fix it so's all the judge would give you was a smack on the hand and a telling-off. For starters, what's your name, and who set you up?'

The fellow cleared his throat, wriggled his shoulders, and talked. 'I'm Bert Stubbings, me mate's Joe Harrington. This chap came into the pub last night. Told us his name was Fred Merlin and as how the bloke as lives here was a crook who'd pinched something what he'd made and was going to pass it off as his own. Gave us a hundred down with five hundred more when we'd got this control box or whatever it was. He was a weedy bloke, with a flat cap and smoky glasses. He had a sore throat, because he talked gruff like,' Bert explained.

'Oh, him,' Brenda chipped in. 'What was he driving, a red Metro or a green Toyota?'

'Didn't see no car,' Bert admitted.

'Merlin, you said he called himself?'

'S'right.'

Walsh looked up at the ceiling and puffed his pipe as near contentedly as he could manage. Unaccountably, the notes from the 'Air on a G string' lilted through his mind.

'Let me have some of last night's surveillance reports on what our prime suspects were up to,' Walsh growled, now back in his office at Headquarters. 'Maybe we can rescue something from this fiasco yet.'

'Well, most of them didn't stir all night, Chief. Not the ones I've read about,' Brenda replied, pushing a sheaf of papers across the desk.

'They weren't under full surveillance, don't forget,' Inspector Kennedy reminded everyone gloomily. 'Any of them could

165

have gone out of their back ways, over a fence or two, and used someone else's car.'

'This Dr John Bailey character went out,' Myres announced.

'What time?' Walsh asked. The so-called Fred Merlin had made his deal with Stubbings and Harrington by nine o'clock.

'Just after ten, and guess where he went?' Myres's question was obviously intended to be rhetorical since he added the answer without pausing. 'He went round to that Dr Anita Grant's, and stayed there the rest of the night, but – here, hang on just a minute. Where's my case?'

The others watched with increasing impatience as Myres dug out a thick wad of routine interview reports and proceeded to flip through them. 'I've only had time to go through them the once,' he explained while he was still reading. 'I like to do that to get the gist of them, so when I read them again I can spot the similarities. Here we are. These are the house-to-house statements on the Ambrose fire-bombing, of course. A fellow in the house on the corner, where the estate joins the main road, reckons he saw a dark sports car that night. An MG he thought it was, but this chap Bailey drives a green Morgan. Mighty similar, a Morgan and an old MG, particularly at night, and there aln't that many of either about at any time of the day. The only thing is, though, this fellow was convinced it had a woman driver. I don't know, but it might be worth following up.'

'You couldn't describe Bailey as a weedy bloke,' Brenda observed, shaking her head.

'Maybe not,' Myres agreed. 'But you looked a weedy bloke when you dressed up as Julian Fry. I haven't seen this Dr Anita Grant, myself, but would she look a weedy chap if she was dressed up as Fred Merlin?'

'She might just do that,' Brenda mused, rubbing her chin thoughtfully.

'And she drives a green Toyota and is an ex-Arthur King lover,' Walsh added. 'I think it might pay us to call on Dr Grant, but before we do, I'll just read these reports myself. Do you think you could organize some coffee, Brenda? Then you can ring Julian Fry in Hughes's rooms at Downing College.

Tell him his house is still nearly all in one piece. He can have it back whenever he wants, although I'd advise him to stay well under cover until the word's got around that the whole thing was a total fiasco. I'll go round and thank him personally, as soon as I can find the time.'

15

Anita Grant frowned and looked irritated when the door bell of her flat rang, and her mind toyed with the idea of ignoring its insistent tone altogether.

She wasn't expecting anyone. There was no point in John Bailey coming for another week, so the chances were that this untimely caller was a fellow resident, out to borrow something rather than take the short trip round the corner to the ever-open shop, or one of the bored ones hoping to be invited in for a drink or a coffee and an hour's meaningless gossip.

She looked at the rows and rows of words displayed before her on the word processor screen. She hated being interrupted at the best of times and this was particularly annoying, because she'd been in full literary flow with this letter to her sister in Montreal.

It was strange that she and her sister had never got on well when they'd been younger; since they'd gone their different ways in the big wide world they'd become *confidantes extraordinaires*, and the more the miles between them so the bulk of detail in their correspondence had increased. Perhaps that was because the social groups in which they each moved consisted largely of cynical sarcastic people, to whom it would not be safe to reveal one's innermost secret thoughts . . .

The bell rang again.

Anita scowled angrily, but her feet had already found her slippers beneath the table and she got up and went to the door.

The man standing there was the police inspector she'd met before, in the lab. He'd reminded her then vaguely of her father, but now the strained look on his face and the hard cold penetrating eyes made that likeness quite uncanny.

'Good evening, Dr Grant,' Sidney Walsh said pleasantly. 'We'd like to come in and have a word with you. There are some points we'd like cleared up, if you could spare the time.'

Anita Grant scowled. This man was already stepping forward, so confident was he that his request would be granted. Presumptuously self-assured men like him were the kind she hated most. Like her father, his manner assumed there would be instant obedience to his will, and that made her feel so damnably small, frightened and insecure. Disobedience when young had meant the humiliation of a smacked backside, but the man standing before her had a high police ranking to give him a power and influence that a wise person would not confront too directly.

She stepped back reluctantly to allow her unwanted visitors to enter, all three of them, for Brenda Phipps and Alison Knott followed Walsh.

'Make yourselves comfortable,' Dr Grant said sarcastically, flopping herself down heavily in one of the easy chairs. 'And what is it that's so important that it couldn't wait for a more civilized time of day?'

Two of her visitors sat on the settee opposite her, but Brenda preferred to stand by the table.

Walsh studied the woman's face for some moments before answering. There was a slight flush to her cheeks and a hint of wildness in her restless eyes, which betrayed an inner mental tension of some kind.

'Well,' he said eventually, 'it appears that a few evenings ago, in the very early hours, you went out for a drive in your friend John Bailey's green Morgan. Would you tell me where you went, and what was the purpose of your journey?'

Anita's heart started pounding fast. Her father used to phrase questions with linked assumptions in that infuriating way. Dare she deny she'd been with John, when it was all too likely that some busybody watcher had seen them leaving the block of flats? Her fingers twisted nervously in her lap. When she was young she had invariably lied, if she felt she could get away with it. It was the only way she could fight her father's restrictive power. She racked her brain for something clever and cutting to say. A straight answer was definitely not acceptable.

'You'd better ask John Bailey. It's his car,' was the best she could do.

'So we shall, but since you were driving the Morgan, we thought we'd ask you first. It's amazing just how many people in a city the size of Cambridge are up and about in the very early hours, and wide awake at that. Morgans are rare cars, too. People remember them. So where did you go, and why?'

Anita's normally agile mind groped helplessly for words. Her eyes widened as she glared at this so-similar reincarnation of the father she had hated. It was as if he were deliberately setting out to humiliate her in front of these other two gloating women. Her mother might have escaped by throwing a tantrum and hurling things about, but such behaviour wouldn't work against the police. Nothing could be worse than having to admit the truth; but the truth was the only ambiguous answer she could think of.

'I don't know where we went,' she blurted out.

'We? So Bailey was with you, was he? If you were just out for a spin, why didn't he drive, or did he give you directions?' Walsh questioned remorselessly.

This was almost unbearable. He was twisting her back on to the barbs of her own words.

'John said I could drive. There's no harm in that, is there?' she said defiantly, blinking back the tears of frustration that were starting to form.

'None at all, but what happened when you stopped in Docking Drive?'

'I don't know anything about Docking Drive.'

'But you stopped somewhere, didn't you? What happened then?'

Anita shrugged helplessly. The police knew so much, but

how much? There were plenty of good reasons why they might have stopped, there was no need to deny that.

'Sure we stopped, but I don't know where that was. John had some letters to post. He'd left them in the car, you see, and forgotten them. John's not very good at remembering things –'

'But he is bloody good in bed, isn't he?' Brenda's voice interrupted sharply from by the table. 'Just listen to this lot, Chief,' she said, reaching forward to scroll up the cursor of the word processor to bring the beginning of the page into view.

'Hey, you leave that alone, you nosy bitch,' Anita screamed in fury, jumping to her feet while the tears began to roll down her cheeks. 'That's bloody private! You leave it alone.' As quickly as she had moved, she found the stocky solid figure of Alison Knott barring her way.

'Sit down, Dr Grant. Control yourself, please,' Walsh ordered calmly. 'Go on, Brenda.'

'This is what it says, Chief,' Brenda announced. '"I've got a new one, you know. This John came round the other night and, jeepers, he does it like a raging rampant bloody bull. Head down and the charge. When he'd finished I was near black and blue all over, and sore as hell. Now, you take your darling sister's advice, and find yourself a rampant bull, and you'll have a lovely sleepless night. But only once a week, it takes that long to get over it." The important bit's coming next, Chief,' Brenda went on.

'It's not fair, it's not fair,' Anita cried, drumming her fists on the arm of her chair.

'"This John's not all there up top, though. I told you, didn't I, that Arthur had been murdered. Well, at the lab we think it's someone in the animal rights movement who did it. So, what does my stupid bull get it in his thick head to go and do? He got me to drive his car while he put a petrol bomb through one of their letter boxes. I didn't know that until the next day, but two little girls damn near died. His brains aren't in his head they're in his –" Well, never mind the rest, Chief,' Brenda went on. 'There's enough here to have her as an accomplice in attempted murder, at least.'

'Can you save what's on the screen, Brenda, and see if there's any older letters in the memory disc? Maybe there's more about Arthur KIng's murder,' Walsh asked. 'Alison, radio through to HQ, and find Reg. I want an official search warrant for this place – Packstone's team can give it a through going over – and we'll have the fellow that does the identikit pictures. He can do some sketches of Dr Grant with a flat cap and tinted spectacles. Maybe we'll find we've got Fred Merlin. Then we'll go and bring this John Bailey in. I hope he resists – we wouldn't mind having a go at a bloody rampant bull who nearly killed two innocent little girls, would we, Alison?' Walsh glared remorselessly at Anita Grant. 'I don't suppose the solicitor you use will be very pleased at being called out, but I strongly advise you to have him here. You're in trouble, Dr Grant. Serious trouble.'

Confused and frightened, the tough, independent Dr Anita Grant reverted to her childhood way of confronting authority, by drumming her hands on the arm of the chair and her heels on the floor, then suddenly she buried her face in her hands, and began sobbing and crying hysterically.

'She's not in a fit state to be questioned any further,' the doctor said, looking worried and harassed as he closed Anita Grant's bedroom door behind him. 'In any case, I've given her a strong sedative. She'll sleep for six to eight hours now. I must say, Inspector, I consider she's been put under the most extreme mental pressure. She's normally so very stable and in control of herself.' He glared accusingly at Walsh, but fired his final reproving glance at the grey-suited solicitor who was seated on the settee patiently studying his fingernails. 'Your presence is supposed to prevent such things, Martin,' he went on angrily. 'What the hell do you think you're playing at?'

Obviously the two were acquainted.

The solicitor shrugged his shoulders complacently. 'She was like that when I got here, George. I insisted you were called straight away.'

'Was she so? Well, you did the right thing, then. What's it all about? What's she supposed to have done anyway?' the doctor demanded of Walsh.

'Nothing much. She's only involved in fire-bombing a house and nearly killing two little girls,' Walsh snapped, plainly nettled, 'and possibly she's involved in two rather brutal murders as well.'

The doctor looked shocked and astounded. 'Good lord! Well, perhaps I can understand your questioning being, a bit, er, over-enthusiastic, but I warn you, Inspector, you're not going to do any more a strong-arm stuff with my patient. She's already been put in a state of complete hysteria and until her mental state is stabilized she should have someone with her all the time. Hysteria can be followed by a deep depression that can result in a suicidal mood, you know. Then you'd really be in trouble. I'll come back in the morning, but she stays under my care. No further questioning until I say so. Is that understood?'

'Perfectly, doctor. Thank you for coming,' Walsh answered as politely as he could.

'And no questioning without me being present to ensure that you keep your interrogations within the law that you're supposed to be upholding, Chief Inspector,' the solicitor demanded as he also got up to leave. 'Really, if you're planning to present the words displayed on a word processor screen as evidence in court, then I'm going to have a field day with you,' he smirked.

Walsh turned away to go and talk to Richard Packstone.

'Trouble?' Packstone asked.

'Blasted woman got the screaming ab-dabs.'

'He'll drop you right in it, if you're not very careful,' Packstone warned, but whether that referred to the doctor or the solicitor was not clear, and Walsh could not be bothered to find out. He felt that he'd had more than enough distractions. Maybe he'd found the murderer of Arthur King and Elizabeth Asher in either Grant or Bailey. They were both on his suspect list as King's ex-lover and her new lover. That provided a tentative motive, but he needed real proof, incontrovertible proof against either of them. Something that would stand up to pressure in a court of law. So far, all was supposition. The acid test was not whether those two hoodlums from Fry's house might recognize a sketch of Grant with glasses and flat cap as the Fred Merlin who had set them up, but how the hell whoever really was Merlin had managed to magic himself in and out of Arthur King's house without activating the burglar alarm. Everything really hinged on that, even if Packstone and the search teams could find some other direct link. All he'd achieved so far, other than the naming of two fire-bombers, was the identification of two simple-minded animal lovers, whose sole crime, other than a dubious conspiracy to commit an offence, was failing to report a minor motor accident, and the apprehension of two other simple-minded vicious thugs – one of whom was still in intensive care and whose lawyer would soon, no doubt, be joining Anita Grant's doctor, and screaming loud and long about police brutality.

There were times when this job of looking after and protecting the general public seemed to involve fighting them as well as the criminally minded.

'Are you expecting us to find anything in particular?' Packstone asked, watching the other's face intently.

Walsh was definitely showing signs of stress with those uncontrolled facial movements, and if that strain was not relieved in some way, there could be serious problems. He'd have a quiet word with the Chief Constable when Walsh was out of the way. The CC would ease the pressure before any damage was done.

'A flat cap, tinted glasses, a key that fits King's door, garrotting wire, alarm system data, anything that might link her in with the two murders,' Walsh said irritably. 'Then, when you've done here, Richard, there'll be her boy-friend Bailey's place to go over as well. We'll interview him down at the station, with his solicitor and a dozen bloody good men as witnesses, just in case he decides to throw a damned wobbly as well.'

'You'll be at it all night then,' Packstone muttered. 'I think

you ought to try and get some shut-eye, Sidney. You're looking
a bit tired, if you don't mind my saying so.'

'I don't mind what you say, Richard, but I'll take my breaks
only when I can let my own team off the hook, and at the
moment I haven't the slightest idea when that will be.'

'He's tougher than Grant was, boss,' Reg Finch said, resting his
bandaged hand on the table, and rubbing his tired eyes with the
other. 'He's admitting they went out for a drive that night, and
that he got out to post some letters, but that's all. Says he'd
never heard of Docking Drive or the Ambroses. That's about
the only mistake he's made, since we can prove both the name
and the address are on that list of animal rights activists the
laboratory had compiled, but even so, I don't see that's got us
very far,' he went on gloomily.

Walsh started pacing the room. Nothing was ever neatly cut
and dried, certainly, but he'd been over and over things in his
mind, and he was certain that he was following the only logical
course of action. It was obvious that the Ambrose bombing
had to be linked with the two murders, and he'd be criminally
incompetent if he didn't act as though that was the case. Having found a weak spot in the murderer's defences, he needed
to throw in every last ounce of his reserves and energies. Only
then would his enemy's lines falter and collapse.

The telephone rang.

'Sidney,' the CC's voice sounded clipped and precise, 'I've
had some complaints about you and what you're doing. I want
to see you in my office at ten o'clock tomorrow morning. In the
mean time, you're to hand over whatever's going on to either
Finch or Kennedy, and you're to go home and get some rest.
Take a sleeping pill if necessary. That's an order. Do you hear
me? Right?'

This was an unexpected flank attack. Walsh's own big guns
had suddenly been turned against him. With almost the whole
world opposing him it was high time to withdraw into his shell.
The fight could continue another day.

'Right,' Walsh confirmed reluctantly.

Fortunately sleep came readily in the cold bed of his silent house. He dozed off as soon as his head touched the pillow, and he remained that way, undisturbed, until his alarm went off next morning.

'Well, I'm surprised anything came from your ambush plan at all, Sidney,' the CC said agreeably, leaning his elbows on the desk and carefully placing his hands together as though in prayer. Then he rested his chin on his extended fingers to study Walsh's face intently.

His Serious Crime investigator did look tired, but not excessively so now. Last night's sleep, or at least, undisturbed rest, had probably done him good. He had not doubted the wisdom in Packstone's advice that Walsh was pressing himself too hard, for Packstone was a wily old bird who knew a thing or two about stress symptoms. There was no implied criticism of Walsh's behaviour: on the contrary, in any battle, whether military or against crime, an officer of a field unit needed to go all out to exploit any weakness in the enemy's lines. That was how battles were won. At the same time, however, a general commanding officer needed to keep a clear head, to stand back from the smoke and clash of arms, in order to get a clear view of the ground and to properly direct his forces. The fact that Walsh was trying to do both jobs, fight in the lines as well as direct a battle, was, in part, a fault of the constabulary's operational command structure. Sustained action was bound to cause stress. It was the Chief Constable's job to relieve that strain when it became excessive.

'So, while this chap was trying to bash young Brenda Phipps's head in with a hammer, Reg Finch comes in with a bare fist uppercut that lays the fellow out cold and breaks his jaw – and dislocates Finch's knuckle into the bargain. Nothing wrong with that, by God. I wish I could have seen it. It must be nice to be in a bit of action rather than be stuck behind a blasted desk like mine all the time. You called the ambulance pretty well straight away, you say? Good work. There's nothing contradictory in any of the reports? Right, no problems there. We can't be faulted. I'll deal with any further complaints on that score. Now, this woman Anita Grant,' the CC went on, changing his position by leaning back in his chair. 'Who was with you when you questioned her? Ah, no. You weren't questioning her with a charge in mind at the time, were you? You were just conducting a normal interview in the pursuance of your inquiries. So we can say there was no need for her solicitor to be there at that time. Phipps and Knott went with you? Two women, that's even better. So she went bananas when Phipps read out the letter she'd written to her sister saying that she drove the car while Bailey delivered the petrol bomb. I'll scotch that one by complaining to the Law Society that one of their members is making accusations without ascertaining the true facts. Right, that deals with all that. Now, I understand Packstone's lot haven't found anything yet to link Grant or Bailey with King's or Asher's murders. What are you going to do now?'

'It looks as if I'll have to go back to the basics,' Walsh replied calmly. 'More interviews, rechecking existing statements. I'll spend today going through all the files again, and outline a new plan. There are a few minor points that haven't been fully followed up yet, and there's a whole load of stuff in the files Kennedy, Ackers and Myres have prepared.'

The CC smiled cheerfully. There now seemed nothing to be worried about. 'That's right – after a bit of action you need to regroup, deal with casualties, do a bit of maintenance and check your supplies. Then you'll be ready for further manoeuvres. Gwen'll be back in a day or so, you say? I won't mind if you have a day or two off to be on your own together – do you good – but the last thing you must do at this stage in the investigation is go charging blindly off on another wild-goose chase. Right?'

'Right.'

It was shortly after lunch when the telephone on Walsh's paper-strewn desk rang.

'Inspector, how are you?' came Professor Edwin Hughes's cheerful deep voice.

'I'm very well, Professor. How are you?' Walsh replied politely.

'Fine, fine. Julian and I have just come back from his house in Ely. He needed his other dinner jacket. The one he brought with him got rather messed up in the common room last night. So did mine, as a matter of fact. We haven't had so much fun in years.' He chuckled. 'However, none of that is to the point, my boy. While we were in his house he came upon that little problem you'd left there, the one you've been having with your alarm system.' There was the distinct sound of laughter in the background. 'Oh, all right, Julian. Have it your own way, you tell him.'

'Inspector, I'm an independent computer systems consultant. That's how I make my living, you know. So if you want the answer to your problem, I'll have to make a charge,' Julian Fry said, then he burst into deep raucous laughter.

An icy tingle ran down Walsh's suddenly tensed spine. 'I don't care how much you charge,' he gulped. 'What's the answer? –' but the phone had gone dead. Fry had rung off.

Walsh's fingers trembled as he put the receiver down. His first instinctive reaction was to ring back immediately, but there was something about that laughter that stopped him. Fry and the professor both sounded as though they had been imbibing the brandy rather too freely, but no, it wasn't that. What the hell was it? He put his head in his hands and closed his eyes.

'Are you all right, Chief?' Brenda Phipps asked in concern.

Walsh ignored her.

It was as though his mind was going into a spin, with his thoughts rushing about in confusion. 'If you want the answer to your problem, I'll have to make a charge.' What the hell was so funny about that?

The thoughts in his mind seemed to slow down and sort themselves out into some sort of order. What did he know about that damned alarm system in Arthur King's house? He conjured up a picture of Packstone and Jim MacDunn the

177

installer, when they were in the kitchen of King's house, while that blasted mind-numbing bell was still ringing. What had they been saying, or was it one of the later conversations?

Suddenly he realized that he had the last and most vital clue. The one he'd most wanted – the one he'd expected the experts to give him. It had provided the answer he'd been searching for. Now he knew who had killed Arthur King, and how it had been accomplished. He didn't yet know for certain why, but he could reasonably guess the motive. He got up and paced about the room.

'Right in front of our noses all the time,' he muttered to himself.

'What? What is it?' Reg Finch and Brenda demanded in unison.

'In a minute. In a minute. Your files, Brenda, let me have them.'

He flipped through the pages and read a list, but the name he wanted to see wasn't there.

The warning by the CC about not chasing any more wild geese passed momentarily through his mind, but he'd opened up a great hole in his enemy's lines. If he struck now, with a determined all-out assault, the battle would be over, and victory would be his.

He picked up the phone, and dialled a number. 'Mr MacDunn,' he said. 'This is Chief Inspector Walsh, I'd like to . . .'

16

They did not need to go far. It was a journey that was best accomplished on foot.

'We've got to move very carefully indeed,' Walsh explained as they hurried out of the Police Headquarters building in Parkside, Cambridge, and turned left, to walk up to the roundabout, and then left again along the busy East Road. 'We know Fred Merlin's mighty jumpy. Anything suspicious, anything out of the ordinary, might make him run for it or do something equally stupid; and nothing would make him panic quicker than the sight of police uniforms all over the place. So we'll have to do the job ourselves.'

'The trouble with a place like this,' Reg Finch said, nodding towards the extensive buildings of brick, glass and concrete on the other side of the road, 'is that they're so big and there's so much going on all the time.'

'The Principal is expecting us. He'll put us right,' Walsh replied confidently, pushing through the swing doors into the entrance foyer of what had once been a humble technical college, but was now a polytechnic, and one with the prospect of becoming an entire university all on its own.

The tall, grey-suited Principal rose from behind his massive uncluttered desk as his visitors were shown into his office.

'Good afternoon, Chief Inspector. I understand you wish to apprehend and question one of our staff. Well, I could wish you not to do it on these premises but I don't suppose that will make you change your mind. Mr Amaris here,' he waved a hand to indicate a younger, shorter man with an eager expression on a rather spotty face, 'who is in charge of that section, will take you to where you wish to go. Classes will be ending in twenty minutes, so if you could wait until the students have left that particular room, I would be most obliged.'

Walsh smiled. 'I'd like us to be standing in the corridor outside. I can see no reason why there should be any problem. Right, Mr Amaris, we'll follow you.'

Mr Amaris chatted politely as he led the way outside, across a wide open quadrangle, towards another block. He really wanted to ask what was going on, but he'd decided that if he stuck around long enough, he'd find out anyway.

Walsh was content to be taciturn and make occasional grunts as his contribution to the conversation. Things, at last, were going well with this Arthur King case.

'That's Block G over there, is it?' he asked, and having received a confirmatory nod he stopped and reached in his pocket for his radio. 'Alison, you and Arthur cover the rear entrance to Block G, just in case. We'll be going to Room 25, on the first floor.'

However, things were not going quite as well with the case as Walsh might have wished. Room 25 on the first floor over-looked the quadrangle, and someone within saw the group below, and recognized the man using the radio.

Without hesitation or delay, that person panicked, grabbed for car keys and ran out of that room, along the corridor and down the stairs.

Walsh was still a few yards away from the Block G main doors as the figure burst out through them and sprinted towards the car-park.

His startled gasp of 'That's who . . .' set Brenda Phipps running after the figure like a bullet from a gun.

So far in this case Brenda had been denied any real physical action, save for the brief encounter with Dr Hammington in the wood, so now was her chance. She was fit and agile, and by the time her quarry had reached the first of the rows of cars in the car-park, she was already close behind.

The figure dodged between the vehicles in a futile attempt to shake off the pursuer, but Brenda wasn't out to play tag games. She leapt up on to the bonnet of a red Metro and thence to the roof of a green Toyota, then bounded over six other cars of various makes, before making a fly-ing dive on to the figure's back. Together they crashed to the ground.

Brenda jumped nimbly to her feet, ready for more action, but the other lay prone on the tarmac, shocked, winded, helpless and dispirited. Regretfully, Brenda found she needed no full nelsons or other wrestling headlocks, but she kept a tight grip on an arm, all the same, as she helped the other to rise.

Walsh shook his head from side to side regretfully.

Jean the puppet-maker's beautiful big blue eyes were full of tears; instead of sparkling with life and humour, as he remembered them. They now expressed sheer terror, and fear, and not a little hate.

* * *

'This is much more like it, Sidney,' the CC said, smiling broadly and rubbing his hands together in great satisfaction at hearing that the two latest serious crimes had both been solved. 'Packstone's lot should come up with something conclusive, even if her verbal confession on tape isn't admissible in court.'

'There's not much for us to do until then,' Walsh admitted seriously. Already the bright euphoria of success was starting to fade into the gloom of anticlimax. Loose ends and legal niceties now needed deep consideration, in a case that only a few hours earlier had seemed light years away from a solution.

Walsh was looking very tired again, the CC decided.

'There's no need for you to hang about now, Sidney. You've done your bit. In fact, what I suggest you do is to take young Phipps and Finch down the pub for a celebration. Put it on expenses. I think our budget can stand that. You've all done very well,' the CC added generously.

Walsh pondered the idea. Drinking was the last thing on his mind, but now he came to think about it, he was hungry.

'We'll go out for a meal, instead,' he said eventually. Then he thought of something else of importance that needed doing as soon as possible. It wasn't going to be merely a courteous gesture, but one expressing the deepest gratitude.

'I'll ring old Professor Hughes in Downing College, first,' Walsh went on. 'After we've eaten I'd like to pop in and say our thanks to Dr Julian Fry. If it wasn't for him we'd still be going through the county's haystacks straw by straw, looking for a needle.'

Professor Hughes's welcome was as effusive as ever. He ushered his guests into his sitting-room and thence to the half-circle of leather-upholstered chairs drawn cosily round the glowing log fire.

'So your murderer is securely under lock and key, Inspector,' Professor Edwin Hughes pronounced with a contented smile as he placed bottles and glasses conveniently for his guests, 'and we can all sleep safely in our beds once again.' Hughes had abandoned his black dinner jacket in favour of one made from a bright tartan material, heavily embellished with gold buttons and braiding: ideal after-dinner wear for someone with a taste for vibrant colours.

Opposite the professor, still in his second-best dinner jacket, sat Dr Julian Lancelot Fry. His silvery-grey locks glistened with sunset-red streaks from the fire's rosy glow, and he had the flushed cheeks and bright eyes of one who had dined and wined very well in college.

Walsh and his two colleagues had perhaps not dined or wined quite so well in the restaurant near Great St Mary's Church, but the meal had enabled them all to unwind and relax.

'To be precise, the murderer is helping us with our inquiries at the moment,' Sidney Walsh smiled. 'Tomorrow we'll apply for a remand in custody, while we tie up the loose ends.'

'Well, tell us all about it then,' Julian Fry demanded, swirling the brandy gently round in his glass. 'All I know is that there was a death-threat letter and a bit about the alarm system's computer.'

'I know that the first victim was a King Arthur enthusiast, but very little else, Julian,' Hughes added.

'It's a rather long and involved story, if you want to hear it from the beginning,' Walsh warned.

'We've rather been looking forward to it, ever since you phoned earlier to say you were coming, haven't we, Julian?' Hughes admitted in happy anticipation.

'In that case I must have your assurances that what is said will be in the strictest confidence, and will not be made available to the press or the public. It might prejudice a fair trial, you see.' Walsh smiled pleasantly. 'I'm sorry, but I have to say that officially.'

'Very understandable. Assurances given,' the professor and Fry said together.

'It's not easy to know just where to start. The beginning was really some years ago,' Reg Finch explained tentatively.

'No, it wasn't, Reg,' Brenda interrupted. 'For us it all began one cold and frosty night, when the snow lay crisp and deep upon the frozen sward,' she went on in a voice that rang with mystery and suspense, 'and out of the misty haze that swirled from distant swamp and murky fen, came the phantom ghostly hound known as Old Shuck.'

'Not a bad start. It certainly has dramatic qualities,' Edwin Hughes acknowledged.

'A dog, I gather, does play some role in these proceedings?' Julian Fry inquired with bushy eyebrows raised.

'Indeed he does,' Reg affirmed, taking up the story. 'A dog wandered for a time through the woods on the far side of the road, before he came to the side door of the house in question, unobserved by the video cameras of the alarm system. It gets a bit confusing then, because the phantom dog suddenly became Merlin, the wizard of King Arthur's day, for that night was to become the last knight of King Arthur. If you'll excuse the witticism . . .'

'Once only,' Julian murmured firmly. 'Just the once.'

'. . . and Merlin entered,' Reg continued.

'Like a real ghost, and straight through the door, I trust,' Hughes chuckled.

Walsh allowed his head to rest against the chair's high back. His stomach felt comfortable and well fed, and the three glasses of wine he'd had with the meal, now with the addition of a few sips of brandy, were making his head swim pleasantly and gently. He was over-tired, and he knew it. He was at the point where his mind was starting to feel detached from his body. This case had been a particularly difficult one, with long periods of stress when he'd felt mentally trapped within the confines of the locked room. Added to that was the fact that he was sleeping badly without Gwen beside him, and even occasionally being woken by her phone calls from the United States. There was also the additional minor pressure of having to feed and look after himself. So, becoming over-tired was all too understandable. However, with that pressure now relieved or coming to an end, he could relax and sit back, and just listen while Reg and Brenda related the tale of Arthur King's death. With humorous additions, they were making it into a passable after-dinner story.

'So this puppet-maker, Jean, sent the death-threat letters hoping to frighten King into having the sophisticated alarm system her boy-friend MacDunn would install,' Julian Fry commented.

'Yes, and that also put more pressure on Mrs King, but the anonymous letter she received, telling her about her husband's affair with Anita Grant, sufficed to get her to leave him,' Brenda pointed out.

'Once she'd got King on his own,' the professor went on, 'and the right alarm system installed in King's house, that completed the killer's two pre-conditions. If it hadn't happened like that, she would probably never have gone ahead with her plans, and King and Asher might still be alive.'

'Probably you're right,' Reg agreed. 'However, she did go ahead, and organized the Dancer brothers next, getting them to pay Arthur King a visit. It wasn't those two who were so important, but Jacko, the Alsatian she knew they'd bring with them. Well, at least the tracks he'd leave. She'd decided that the nearest she could safely get her car to King's house was on the farm track on the other side of the wood. From there she had to pass over soft ground and was bound to leave some tracks, whatever the weather; and snow she could not have expected. So she set out to leave tracks deliberately, with moulded glass-fibre dog's front paw pads on the toes of her shoes, and the hind leg pads on the ends of two sticks.'

'She must have done a lot of practice at pacing out the way a dog walks, because she did it very well,' Walsh interrupted. 'She fooled me, anyway, but there were enough genuine tracks from the Alsatian about to confuse the issue, just as she'd planned. Mind you, if the front video camera had been able to see out as far as the drive and the Volvo, we would have known that the real Alsatian had not in fact gone into King's garden. So the picture would have been clearer from that point of view, if you see what I mean. In the wood the dog tracks circled up to an old oak branch which she used as a bridge. If I'd gone round the other side of that tree, I think I would have picked up the tracks to her car.'

'The Chief's attention was diverted at the time by an elderly medical doctor, who feared he was about to sexually assault her, and so opened fire with her revolver to defend her honour,' Brenda announced with a chuckle.

'Good lord, how exciting,' Hughes exclaimed gleefully. 'That sort of thing never happened to you when you were younger, Julian.'

'The two Dancer brothers might have played a more significant part in confusing the evidence, if they hadn't gone to look in the front window of the house. The killer had inadvertently drawn back the curtains while she was pulling her strings in the hall, setting up the bolt and lock red herring on the inside of the sitting-room door. When the Dancer brothers saw Arthur King lying there on the floor, with the sword Excalibur stuck in him, they promptly panicked and scarpered,' Brenda pointed out.

'Quite understandable too. So should I have done,' Hughes remarked sympathetically. 'Asher presumably provided the duplicate key for the lock on King's side door?'

'That's right. No doubt she took an official laboratory purchase order to a local locksmith and had King's key copied while she was out doing some errand for him in his car,' Walsh explained. 'A sad character, Elizabeth Asher. Her complexes did not make her good company even for other like-minded women, and so she sought companionship, as many lonely people do, in evening classes and sewing circles, where she was always perhaps a little too anxious to help or do good turns. She'd known Jean at the sewing circle for several years. Possibly it was her gossip about all the people in the laboratory where she worked that kept Arthur King in the forefront of Jean's mind, instead of allowing the memories to fade away as they might otherwise have done. Jean was one of the many women Arthur King had hurt emotionally, you see. He'd breached her defences by telling her that he was planning to marry and settle down while awaiting the inheritance of his grandfather's millions. It must have come as a terrible shock to her when he did just that, but with Gwenda Killibury as his wife, not herself. Hot-blooded hatred would be understandable at the time, but even so, I think nothing would have come of it if Asher had not been continuously feeding the cancer with snippets of gossip about what King was up to. However, when the lonely young Scot, MacDunn, the installer of burglar alarms, came on the scene, also seeking companionship as well as knowledge of computer programming, all the weapons for a real bloody vengeance had been delivered into her hands.'

'Elizabeth Asher must have become suspicious about the part she had been playing. What reason had Jean given for wanting the duplicate of King's door key?' Julian Fry asked.

'We don't know, perhaps simply that a joke of some sort was being planned for King's discomfiture,' Brenda suggested, 'but whatever it was, Asher had become a liability, and had to be killed to keep her silent.'

'The fire-bombing had nothing to do with this Jean then, had it?' the professor asked.

'Not directly, but Anita Grant and John Bailey would not have acted as they did if Arthur King had not been murdered,' Walsh pointed out.

'True,' Julian Fry acknowledged, then smiled broadly at Walsh. 'You soon solved my little cryptic clue then, Inspector?'

'Yes, it did dawn on me eventually, but I wish our so-called experts had referred the matter to you much earlier. It would have saved me a lot of worry and heartache,' Walsh said, shaking his head regretfully.

'I doubt if I would have taken it on. I had not, then, met you all, or realized you were friends of this old reprobate of a professor,' Julian Fry replied, waving a hand in the general direction of Hughes's grinning face. 'Tell me though, did you ask MacDunn whether the control box he used for King's system was still in its factory's original, heat-sealed plastic wrappings?'

'Yes, and he said that it was,' Walsh admitted.

'That made the solution more difficult for your experts.

Re-heat-sealing the wrapper well enough to fool someone who was not looking too closely would not have presented your resourceful Jean with much of a problem,' Fry announced positively.

'Certainly not as big a problem as the one we faced,' Walsh added cheerfully. 'Still, when you said you'd have to make a charge for the solution and laughed the way you did, it suddenly dawned on me that you were talking about electrical charges. That could only have meant that if the computer's stand-by batteries were charged up before the control box was installed in the house, then the computer could have held a special program in advance of the official one.' Walsh reached to put his brandy glass down on the highly polished table beside his chair. 'Precisely how it would work, I have no idea,' he admitted, 'but Brenda had told me you were an expert with computer viruses, so I assumed it would be something on similar lines in this case.'

'Would it have been difficult to write a program to upset the way the real alarm system program operated, but only between certain times on certain days, Mr Fry?' Brenda asked.

Fry shook his silvery-grey head and smiled indulgently. 'Not at all. MacDunn had to set the clock so that the time could be displayed on the video recordings. As for the rogue program itself, that would have presented no problems – indeed, there was a maker's manual with the control box which gave all the details of the format of the alarm's true operating program. That was very simple. The first section identified all the sensors that were installed and established their "safe position" signals. Those safe signals provided the standard input into the second section, which contained all the instructions about what the computer should do if the "safe signals" became "warning signals", naturally indicating a contact had been broken and an intruder was on the premises. It might decide to display a warning on the owner's portable master unit, if he was at home; if not, the alarm bell would need to be activated and the police notified. However,' Fry went on, 'all this Jean needed to do was to charge up the computer's stand-by batteries and enter a program which bypassed section one completely, and told the second section that between certain times on certain days, all the signals it received were fixed as "safe signals". Between those times the first section could warn about break-ins as much as it liked – as far as the second section was concerned, everything was all right and safe. So between those times, your Jean could go in and move about just as she pleased. I presume King had some fixed habits, nights when he would always be at home perhaps, that Asher would know about and could have related to his murderer?'

'Yes,' Reg Finch replied. 'King regularly kept one or two nights free each week so that he could get on with his King Arthur book.'

'So, Jean timed her arrival for when the system was to all intents and purposes switched off,' Hughes announced. 'That was why the video cameras were not activated, otherwise you'd have had a picture of her making phantom hound paw prints.'

Walsh smiled and nodded. 'Two things still surprise me though. The first is that the girl's special battery-powered computer program obviously lasted long enough for that unit to be properly installed and connected to the mains; and secondly, that her program could disappear so completely later on that our experts could find no trace of it ever having existed.'

Fry shrugged his shoulders nonchalantly. 'The first is just a matter of timing. She obviously knew his work schedule and had access to anything stored in MacDunn's flat, particularly while he was out, but with a bit of ingenuity she could have kept the batteries charged up indefinitely, by inserting electric probes into the mains input plug through the heat-sealed plastic. It's doubtful whether two tiny holes would ever be noticed. She just had to make sure MacDunn didn't realize what she was up to, and remove her wires just before MacDunn went off to do the final part of the installation.' Fry waited a few moments for heads to nod their comprehension, before he went on. 'Now, as for your second point, her program could have been instructed to wipe itself out at a certain time on a certain day, or this could have been triggered in a different way, perhaps by a certain sequence of numbers being tapped into the control panel. I, personally, would favour the second myself, but whichever way it was triggered, her program would disappear completely. I can assure you of that. There would be no trace left for your experts to find. They were asked the wrong questions, I'm afraid, Inspector,' Fry said with a reproving smile. 'They were asked to find out what was wrong with the installer's program, or with the equipment itself, but there was nothing wrong with any of it, and that's what you were told. Your advisers should have placed all the stuff down and said, work out a way round that lot –'

'Precisely,' Edwin Hughes interrupted, chuckling loudly, 'but you still need a devious mind like Julian's. You know, this has been one of the most entertaining evenings I've had for a long while. Now, I hope you three are not in a hurry to rush away. We've food and drink in plenty, and we should never allow ourselves to become slaves to the passage of time. Like good brandy, good company should be relished and savoured. Besides, we've stories of our own to test your intellectual abilities, haven't we, Julian? Mine's a short one. It starts . . .'

Walsh leaned back in his chair contentedly. The aroma of good brandy wafted from the glass held in his cupped hands. He'd put it down in a minute and fill his pipe. The company here was good and there was nothing to make him want to hurry back to his lonely home. No, a complicated case had been solved and he felt good about that, and Gwen would be home in a couple of days. Life was definitely well worth living.

Brenda looked from Reg's face to the Chief's. Their wives were away, and they seemed relaxed and content enough to while away their time in this sociable atmosphere. There was no reason at all why she shouldn't do the same. Tomorrow was another day anyway – when it came.

These armchair detectives, whether they were college professors or brilliant computer experts, they would never know the real thrills of an investigation, those exhilarating moments of action. Like Reg doing his Tarzan act on Jacko the Alsatian, or his thundering right uppercut in Fry's house, and, indeed, her own flying leap from the roof of the car on to Jean the murderer's back. They were all memories to be savoured and relished, just like the professor's brandy.

Maybe she would finish this glass and have another. She could work any adverse effects off in the gym tomorrow.